Love

And

Chocolate

By Linda Shenton Matchett

Love and Chocolate
By Linda Shenton Matchett

Copyright 2024 by Linda Shenton Matchett. All rights reserved.
Cover Design by: Wes Matchett
Photo Credits:
Woman: Shutterstock/Kateryna Yakovlieva
Warehouse: Ershov Maks

ISBN: 979-8-9877458-7-8

Published by Shortwave Press

Chapter One

Fire crackled in the hearth adding to the stifling heat in the room as Ilsa Krause studied Papa's ledger. No matter how many times she ran the calculation, the result was the same. He had left a tremendous amount of debt and no savings. There wasn't even enough to pay for his funeral. Would the undertaker dig up the grave and retrieve the simple pine coffin to get a portion of the money they owed him?

She sighed and rubbed her throbbing forehead. Her eyes burned from staring at the cramped handwriting of her father, certainly not from crying. She didn't have time for mourning. There was too much to be done.

Being a young man, her brother, Tobias, hadn't cried either. At least not in public. She'd heard him in the barn after the funeral, alternately railing against Papa for dying, and weeping at his absence. Always full of drama, Nadine, of course, had done enough sobbing for all of them, wailing and shrieking when the doctor had pronounced Papa dead from the pneumonia. Hedwig, called Heddie, the youngest of all of them, had mourned in silence, tears trickling down her cheeks.

Perspiration pooled under Ilsa's arms and adhered her bodice to her skin. She could no longer ignore the reality of their situation. The family was not only destitute, but they owed money to most of the merchants in town. How could she have not known the desperation of their circumstances? She'd seen the fatigue and worry in her father's eyes, but assumed his illness was the cause.

"Well?" Tobias's voice cut through the stillness.

Ilsa's gaze shot to her brother, who sat ramrod stiff on the worn upholstered chair, his arms crossed and a frown etching lines on his face. Her glance slid to her sisters, hunched together on the couch, their complexions wan in the dim light of the room. The curtains had been flung open, but gray skies filled with dark, swollen clouds and deepening shadows of the late afternoon did little to brighten Papa's office, a room none of them had been allowed in while he was alive. Now, she knew why. It was easier to hide their dire straits if his children didn't have access to the books.

"It's bad, isn't it?" Heddie's chin trembled. "You have to tell us."

"Yes, just because you're the oldest doesn't mean you're in charge." Nadine's eyes narrowed. "Papa named all of us in the will. We share everything."

"I'm glad you said that, Nadine, because at the moment I feel quite alone in how to proceed." Ilsa licked her lips and smoothed her damp palms on her skirt. "The truth is all that we have to share are bills and financial liabilities."

"That's not possible." Nadine's cheeks paled further. "We have this farm and its income."

Ilsa shook her head. "When the wheat fields failed, Papa mortgaged the farm, and he's only been making minimum payments. Fortunately, he went into dairying ten years ago, which gave him some diversification, but he hated Mr. Beck coming in and buying up so much land for his chocolate factory. Papa refused to sell milk to him. The herd provides for us and a few stores in the area, but the income isn't enough to cover the bills. He's overdue with everyone in town."

"We're poor?" Nadine's eyes bulged. "This is mortifying."

"It's more than—"

"No!" Tobias jumped to his feet and grabbed the ledger from the desk. His lips moved, but no sound came out as he perused the pages. His finger ran down the columns on each page, his expression reddening as the mantel clock ticked the minutes.

Slumped in the chair, Ilsa waited for him to finish, knowing it wouldn't take her intelligent brother long to come to the same conclusion she had. While he flipped through the ledger, she surveyed the room, and her heart constricted.

The faint aroma of Papa's pipe tobacco permeated the air as if he'd been there, but stepped away for a moment. In addition to the chair and sofa, there was a bookcase between the windows. Not much of a reader, her father had filled the shelves with ledgers, papers, and bric-a-brac. The desk was simple, but beautiful. Measuring three feet by six feet, its maplewood surface gleamed, as did the brass hardware on the drawers that flanked the opening. His pride and joy, he'd constructed the piece in the early days of his marriage to Mama.

Mama, who'd been gone for fifteen years from consumption. Her death had left a hole in Papa's life. During the first year after she'd died, he'd barely spoken, going about the farm chores as a man headed for the gallows. Ilsa had taken on the housework and ensured her siblings had clothes to wear and food to eat. He'd eventually come out of the trance but was never the same as he'd been before. The father she knew as a little girl died along with Mama. And now they were orphans.

Tobias tossed the record book on the desk where it landed with a bang, then began to pace. Her sisters flinched, but remained quiet. They knew, as well as she did, not to interrupt his ruminations. Ilsa propped her elbows on the desk and laced her fingers. *Oh, Papa, why didn't you tell us?*

When she thought she couldn't stand Tobias's marching back and forth any longer, he dropped into the chair, his eyes bloodshot and haunted. Turning to Nadine and Heddie, he kneaded his hands. "There's no easy way to say this: We're broke."

Nadine pressed one hand over her mouth, and Heddie sagged against the back of the sofa. Neither girl spoke.

"I don't want to lose the farm." Ilsa spread her hands over the desk. "We owe a lot of people a large amount of money, but I'd like to meet with them and discuss payment plans. The bank, too."

His lips twisted, Tobias said, "Payment plans with what? We have no money, and Papa proved that the little bit we're bringing in from the stores isn't enough."

"There are four of us. We can make this work."

"How?" Heddie's voice trembled.

"Do what Papa wasn't willing to...contract with the factory."

"But that would be going against Papa's wishes." Nadine bolted upright. "How can you consider such a thing?"

Ilsa pinched the bridge of her nose. She'd coddled her sisters and was now paying the price. Their new reality was going to be painful. Would they be able to handle what she proposed? "Papa isn't here, and we have no choice."

"There are always choices." Nadine looked mulish.

"Yes, and one of them is losing everything we own. What do you suggest?"

Her sister shrugged, her gaze riveted on her clenched hands.

Ilsa rose and walked to where Nadine and Heddie sat, then knelt in front of them. It would have been nice to have support from Tobias, but he remained in the chair, head bowed. "Look, we're going to have to make difficult, perhaps terrible decisions, but we need to do what is best for us as a family. I respected Papa, but that doesn't mean I have to like what he did. By being stiff-necked and stubborn, he set us on a path to bankruptcy. We need to reverse that course, and it will mean doing things we may not want to do."

"We could sell the property." Tobias spoke from behind her. "One of the choices is to sell the farm and move to the city."

"And get lousy-paying jobs? Where would we live? In some tenement building that charges too much money for too little space?"

Ilsa winced at the bitterness of her words. "I'm sorry. Yes, that is one of the choices."

"You already have a plan, don't you?" Nadine released a shuddering sigh. "Tell us what you're thinking."

Ilsa glanced over her shoulder at Tobias. His broad shoulders were hunched forward, his hands fisted. Face blotchy, his eyes were clouded as he stared at her. She swallowed a sigh, then patted her sister's leg, and climbed to her feet. She leaned against the desk and crossed her arms. "We work the farm to our best ability. We move from wheat to corn or perhaps split the fields and plant both. One of us, probably Tobias because he's a man, should approach the company and ask for a contract to supply milk. We work with our creditors." She forced a smile. "And those of us who can, get jobs."

"Jobs?" Nadine's eyes widened.

"Yes, jobs. We need outside income, money that isn't dependent on the farm."

"But we only know the farm."

"There are plenty of places that offer unskilled positions. We could wash dishes at one of the restaurants or take in laundry. Some of the shops might be willing to take one or more of us on. How hard can it be to sell products people are looking for?"

"I could work at one of the ranches or farms." Tobias rubbed the back of his neck. "Perhaps one of the bigger places needs a hand."

"No." Ilsa pursed her lips. "You need to take care of our farm. The girls and I will secure the jobs, and we can share the household tasks."

"You haven't mentioned working at the factory. They're always hiring." He cocked his head, a sad smile curving his lips. "If we're going against Papa's wishes, we may as well go all the way."

Nadine wrinkled her nose. "The factory? No. It's too dirty."

"And farm work isn't?"

"Well, yes, but—"

Tobias held up his hands. "I think for now we should talk to our creditors, then try to get a contract with Mr. Beck. I will stay on the farm while Ilsa applies at the factory. We should split up, not all work at the same place, so the girls should see about finding jobs in town. Like we talked about, you know, at one of the shops."

Nadine huffed a sigh. "I agree. We can't all work at the factory. What if it fails? We'd all be out of jobs."

"I'm getting married," Heddie said.

"What?" Ilsa's head snapped up, and she gaped at her sister, her mind racing. "Who? Since when?"

"Since Papa is gone." Heddie cleared her throat. "Billy O'Connell. He asked for my hand, and Papa said no. He wouldn't let us court."

"And now I'm saying no." Tobias rubbed the back of his neck. "He's not one of us."

Eyes blazing, Heddie jumped to her feet. "How dare you say that. You're as closed-minded as Papa. Billy and I love each other. We're both believers, and we're getting married. I'm of age, and you can't stop me."

"But he's Methodist," Tobias sputtered.

"Yes, he is, and you make it sound like a vile thing." She jabbed her finger at him. "We have discussed our beliefs and agree on the important ones. Most of the others are manmade logistics. We're getting married on Friday and leaving town on Saturday. He's gotten a job in Boston, near his family."

Ilsa's stomach hollowed. "You were going to elope, weren't you?"

"Yes." Tears pooled in her eyes. "I don't want to argue about this. Please be happy for me. And stop treating me like a child. I'm as much an adult as the rest of you, despite being the youngest. Besides, you'll have one less mouth to feed. I'll talk to Billy about sending money from his paycheck."

"No." Tobias strode to Heddie and pulled her into an embrace. "You, baby sister, are all grown up. I've refused to admit it, but you're a smart, beautiful young woman who deserves a chance at happiness. You and Billy keep your money. You'll need it to begin your new life." He kissed her cheek. "And I hope you'll allow me the honor of giving you away at the wedding."

As Nadine rose and joined Tobias and Heddie in the hug, Ilsa walked to them on stiff legs, fighting the pinpricks of jealousy that stabbed her. She should have been married years ago, but Ernst had gone off to college, then decided she wasn't good enough for him. A simple farm girl. And now she was too old, destined to be the quintessential spinster hunched over a machine until her joints were bent and swollen.

Chapter Two

"That was an excellent meal, Mother." Ernst Webber swallowed the last of his water, then set down the glass with a thump. "I missed your cooking."

She beamed at him as she swatted his arm. "You're just glad you're no longer fending for yourself, but I appreciate the compliment nonetheless."

His father chuckled. "She's got you there, son."

"Perhaps." Ernst grinned. "But it is good to be home. I enjoyed college and considered staying in Green Bay, but the city is too large, too crowded." He frowned. "Too dirty. Give me clean country air."

"Might not be clean for long with that factory of yours." Father leaned back in his chair. "Mr. Beck has been very successful, and rumors say he's going to expand."

"I'm sure he will at some point. He seems quite ambitious. During my interview, he discussed competing with the European companies that are selling in the United States. I think he'd like to get ahead of them."

"He has a good chance of it. His chocolate bars are delicious and affordable. But to go against his home country doesn't seem right."

Ernst fiddled with his napkin. "But he's an American now. Mr. Beck tried opening a business in Germany, a few times, but couldn't seem to gain a foothold, even after apprenticing with some of the best German chocolatiers. He decided to try his hand here, and as you can see, it was the right decision. Being in the heart of dairyland is perfect."

"Some people say he's building an empire. Purchasing all that land and creating his own town. Cocoaville. What kind of a name is that? Burton was good enough."

"He's trying to create a sense of community."

"We already had a community."

"Anton," his mother broke in. "We should be proud of Ernst. He graduated with honors and has secured a good job with a growing company. What more could we ask for our son?"

His father nodded. "True. I am proud of you, Ernst. Not just for what you've accomplished, but how you comport yourself." He looked over his spectacles. "However, you've missed more than a few Sundays at church. Faith should be the center of your life, not an afterthought."

Ernst's face heated. His father's expression reminded him of the few times he'd been called to the principal's office during high school. Although short and slender, the man had held a formidable bearing. "Yes, Father, but it's important that I make a good impression. I was asked to work in order to set up the department. We're now in full operation, so weekends are my own again."

"It's more important to make an impression on the Lord. He is the only one you should worry about pleasing."

"And I hope He understands when my earthly boss needs me."

"I—"

"No more arguing." Mother held up her hands. "Anton, Ernst knows his relationship with God takes precedence." She winked at her son. "And I look forward to having him worship with us on Sunday."

"Yes, Mother." He swallowed a sigh. Life with his parents would never change. Father expected his opinion to be adhered to, without thought to anyone else's views, and Mother would always be the peacemaker. Perhaps he should speak to Mr. Beck about what sort of housing was available. Mother was right. He was a man now. One who should be living on his own, not with his parents.

"Help me clear, and then we'll have dessert. I made a strudel."

"You know the way to my heart." He climbed to his feet and collected the soiled dinner plates, then followed her into the kitchen. "I thought I smelled cinnamon when I came home."

She lifted one eyebrow. "I'm not the one who should be in your heart. You haven't been to see Ilsa Krause since you've been back."

"I've been busy. You know that."

"Too busy to see your sweetheart?" Mother rinsed the dishes and piled them in the sink. She made quick work of putting away the leftovers, then cut three generous slices of strudel and slid them onto plates. She handed him one and picked up the other two. "Have you and Ilsa had a falling out?"

"She's not my sweetheart, and I don't want to talk about it."

She pursed her lips, then pivoted and marched into the dining room. "What happened? She's a wonderful girl and would make you the perfect wife."

He trudged to his chair, then sank into the seat. "Can we go back to arguing about my working on Sundays?"

"That can't be good." Father grinned and cocked his head. "What is she badgering you about?"

"My love life. Actually, my absence of a love life."

His father grinned and cut a piece of strudel. "Ah, my little *heiratsvermittlerin*. Give the boy some time. He'll find his way. It took you and me a while to realize we were meant for each other."

"I'm not a matchmaker." She took a sip of coffee. "He already had the girl, and now he's lost her. I don't understand how he could change his mind about her. They were so in love."

"He is young. There is plenty of time for him to marry."

Ernst waved his hands. "Could you not talk about me as if I were absent? Mother, I know you mean well, and maybe Ilsa and I will get back together, but for the time being, I want to focus on my career."

His mother huffed a breath and poked a bite of strudel into her mouth. She was not happy with him, but it couldn't be helped. He definitely needed to see about moving out.

"Have you visited the family since returning?" Father stabbed at his dessert. "You know her father passed away, yes? You should at least pay a condolence call."

Squirming in the chair, Ernst studied his plate. Father was right. He should have stopped by the house to express his sympathy at their loss, but he'd shied away from going because he thought she'd throw him out. Literally. Truth be told, he was a coward. He'd been thrilled to work on Sundays and avoid church...and his former girlfriend. "Yes, sir."

Four years had passed since he'd looked upon her face. Had she changed? Grown more beautiful? Or had working the farm aged her? Guilt pricked his heart. Looks weren't everything. In fact, he'd fallen in love with her fiery spirit and stalwart faith. But his love had been that of a boy, not the mature feelings of a man.

Attending college changed him. He'd seen things she couldn't imagine. He'd lived in the city. She was country born and bred. Her beliefs were provincial, taking everything the Bible said as absolute. But he'd met people who expanded his mind, showing him the error of his thoughts. They'd debated the finer points of the stories found in the Bible, and he'd determined that's exactly what they were...stories. Fables to guide men and women in their daily lives. His parents believed as Ilsa did and would be horrified at his new philosophies. Another reason to move out. Not only had he outgrown his high school sweetheart, but Mother and Father, too.

Chapter Three

Heart pounding, Ilsa followed the chattering, laughing, and jostling men and women into the factory. Inside, they split up, the men streaming down one hallway, the women another. She hesitated and tightened her grip on her pocketbook, palms moist. Several women who looked as uncertain as she felt, huddled together against one wall. She lifted her chin and walked toward them. "Are you new?"

They nodded as one.

"I—"

"Ladies! My apologies for keeping you waiting," a male voice boomed over the noise.

She whirled to see Mr. Bauman, the man with whom she'd interviewed, striding across the tiled expanse, a broad smile on his face. His bald pate glistened with perspiration, his spectacles perched on the end of his nose.

"Welcome to Beck's. We're so pleased you decided to join us." He swept his arm toward a door she hadn't noticed during the mayhem. "We must keep the accountants happy, so we'll go in there to complete your paperwork, and I will explain how we operate."

Like ducklings, Ilsa and the other women trailed behind Mr. Bauman. He opened the door and motioned them inside. She gaped at her surroundings. Painted powder-blue above the white chair rail, and navy blue below, the walls held ornately framed artwork of serene landscapes that made her feel as if she were looking out a window. Set up like a classroom, there were several rows of tables and chairs. The air smelled of chocolate, a smooth, sweet aroma that filled her nose and caused her stomach to rumble. She'd been unable to choke down any breakfast because of nerves.

"Have a seat, ladies." He beamed at them from the front of the room like a benevolent teacher. "We have much to accomplish, and your supervisors are anxious for you to begin." He distributed several sheets of paper and explained each one. For several minutes the only sound in the room was that of pencils scratching across the pages. He collected their papers, tossed them on the desk, then stuffed his hands into his pockets and rocked on his heels, excitement sparkling in his eyes. Each morning you will head to the locker rooms where you may stow your personal effects. You will then pass through a room that holds head coverings similar to the mob caps of old which cover your hair completely. Then you will don a white coat to protect your street clothes. Your next stop will be the handwashing station. Depending on the nature of your job, you will be issued gloves."

He exhaled. "As we walk through the factory, you will experience Mr. Beck's brilliance in designing the facility for utmost efficiency.

Deliveries of milk, cocoa beans, sugar, and other raw materials are made at the western end of the building where they are taken to their assigned rooms for processing. Once completed, the items move to the next station in the procedure, and so on. By the time you arrive at the eastern end of the factory, you are in the finishing area, where the bars and other chocolate items are inspected, wrapped, and packaged for shipping."

Ilsa raised her hand. "How many bars are produced per day, Mr. Bauman?"

He bestowed a look as if she were a star pupil and had just provided a solution for flying to the moon. "I'm glad you asked. We've only been in operation for six months, but our output is second to none with tens of thousands of pieces being manufactured each day. That number will be increasing when the new machine arrives."

"As I said before, welcome. Mr. Beck values each of you and appreciates your willingness to work for his company. He wants you to be happy, which is why he has gone to great lengths at creating this town and all its support structures. As employees, you have access to shops, doctors, a library, an indoor pool, a playground, and two theaters. You will be issued an identification card that you must show in order to avail yourself of the benefits."

One of the girls behind Ilsa mumbled something, and Mr. Bauman pierced with her a razor-sharp glare. "Do you have a question or comment?"

"Uh, no, sir."

Ilsa laced her fingers and shuddered. Apparently, the man's jovial attitude was a farce as perhaps his claim that Mr. Beck wanted everyone to be happy. Good to know. No matter. She'd settle for a paycheck and a chance to pay off Papa's debt.

"All right, then gather your things, and we'll tour the facility." He gathered their paperwork, then led the women from the room and down the corridor to the locker room. He waited for them to stow their personal items, obtain a jacket and head covering and clean their hands before guiding them through the manufacturing plant at a rapid pace, peppering them with information as they walked. He pointed to various machines and explained their usage.

Ilsa was nearly out of breath by the time they arrived at the far end of the factory in the shipping department. Workers scurried among towers of boxes, grabbing the cartons and loading them onto waiting wagons where they would be taken to the train station for their journey to the rest of the country. She'd heard men at one of the shops in town discussing Mr. Beck's distribution process, indicating it was as efficient and effective as his factory layout.

Mr. Bauman clapped his hands. "Time to go to work, ladies." He ushered them back the way they'd come, then entered a massive area where dozens of women sat at tables or stood in front of machines wrapping products. A diminutive man with snow-white hair waved from the far end of the room. "Miss Krause, Miss Gutnik, and Miss Jasinski, this is your assigned department. Mr. Davison is your supervisor. He will train you on your duties and answer any questions you have. You will receive a fifteen-minute break in the morning and afternoon, and one forty-five-minute lunch period. Your coworkers will show you where the ladies' dining room is located. Good luck." He turned on his heel and disappeared through the doorway.

While waiting for Mr. Davison to finish what he was doing, Ilsa surveyed the room. The ceiling soared overhead with windows near the tops of the walls, enabling light into the area but no view. As with the entire factory, the scent of chocolate permeated the air so heavily she almost felt as if she could taste the products. Would she tire of the aroma?

"Ladies, welcome!" Mr. Davison trotted toward them, his face wreathed in smiles.

Swallowing a sigh, Ilsa straightened her spine at the sound of his British accent. Would he be like Mr. Bauman, gracious one minute and dictatorial the next?

"Let's get you situated. I've paired you each with an experienced gal. The machines are not much more difficult to run than your sewing machines at home, but they can be tricky for the uninitiated."

"I'd like to see him run my sewing machine," Miss Gutnik whispered.

Mr. Davison snickered, and the woman blushed to the roots of her hair. "Sorry," she mumbled.

"No need to apologize, my dear. You're spot on. I'd probably get all tangled up. I was merely trying to set your minds at ease, letting you know that you're already ahead of the game with transferable experience."

Ilsa sighed, and some of the tension slipped from her shoulders. Perhaps he was a nice man after all. He'd reacted with humor instead of ire.

"Miss Krause, you'll be working with Miss Petric." He motioned toward a tall, buxom woman with gray eyes and sandy-brown hair. Her skin was fair with a smattering of freckles on her nose.

The woman lifted her hand in greeting. "It is nice to meet you. Please call me Zlata."

"I am Ilsa." She licked her lips as Mr. Davison moved away with Miss Gutnik and Miss Jasinski, taking them to machines at the far end of the room. The only women she'd come to know in her short tenure were too far away to converse with. Not that she'd have time to talk, but seeing a familiar face would be nice. "I've never done anything like this."

Zlata laid her hand on Ilsa's arm. "You'll be fine. It is less difficult than your sewing machine."

"That's what Mr. Davis said, but I hesitated to believe him. These monstrosities are much larger."

"How the mighty have fallen," a voice sounded from the next machine. "Never thought I'd see you darken the doorway of Beck's, Ilsa. Your father thought he was too good to work with the company."

She glanced over her shoulder. Yasmina Carle smirked, her eyes like black marbles. For some reason Ilsa could never fathom, the girl had been nasty to her since their first meeting in grade school. She'd gotten worse in high school, and Ilsa had been relieved to graduate, after which she'd never seen Yasmina again. Now, she'd be expected to work next to her. *Dear God, help me be kind and not respond to her rudeness.* "Nice to see you again, Yasmina." She spoke through gritted teeth.

"Yeah, right." Yasmina looked down her nose at Ilsa. "I'd heard your father died and left you in a mess. Guess the rumor was right."

"Be quiet, Yasmina." Zlata frowned. "Go back to work."

"I don't have to listen to you."

"Is everything all right, ladies?" Mr. Davison had approached unheard because of the noise of the machines. His gaze shot back and forth between Zlata and Yasmina.

"Fine, Mr. Davison. Ilsa and I are getting reacquainted." Yasmina's voice was syrupy. "We were schoolmates."

Ilsa stifled the desire to roll her eyes, instead nodding as if in full agreement. Any other response might label her as a troublemaker.

He studied them for a long moment, then shrugged and sauntered off.

A glance at Yasmina showed she'd already returned to her machine, but her stiff stance spoke volumes. The conversation was not over.

"Don't let her bother you. She's miserable and thinks everyone else should be, too." Zlata laid her hand on Ilsa's arm. "Now, let's get you trained." She pointed to various parts on the machine as she explained how to operate the apparatus. "You watch for a while, then I will let you try. The noise can be intimidating, but there is nothing to fear. Before we start, we'll need to fill the hopper with the wrapping sheets. Inventory is kept on the shelves at the end of the room. Each product is covered with a different color paper, and we want the blue papers for this product."

Tugging at her cap, Ilsa lifted her chin and strode down the aisle between the machines, a barrage of noise pummeling her from all sides. She arrived at the shelf, grab a large stack of blue tissue-like paper, then spun around to return to her station.

"Oof."

Two strong hands gripped her upper arms. Warmth penetrated the thin fabric of her sleeves, and tingles shot from her elbows to her shoulders. She raised her head and gasped. "Ernst!"

"Ilsa."

His tone was soft as his lips formed her name, but his eyes bulged. "I didn't realize you are employed with us. Uh, I'm sorry for your loss. I heard about your father."

"Thank you." Her mouth dried, and her tongue stuck to the roof of her mouth. He looked good. Too good, but she couldn't allow her heart to follow that trail. He had shunned her, and she would do the same. She glanced at his hands still grasping her arms, and he released her as if burned.

"I-I'm surprised to see you," he stammered.

Her cheeks warmed, but she glared at him. "I didn't have a choice; however, that's no longer any of your business. I must return to my station." She pressed her lips together, pushed past him, and strode down the aisle. Her pulse skittered. Would she have to see him every day? Multiple times per day? Could her life get any worse?

##

"Ilsa, wait." Ernst hurried to catch up with his former girlfriend. "Please, give me a moment."

She stopped but didn't turn around. Her shoulders were square and stiff, her spine ramrod straight.

He slipped past, then pivoted so he could face her. "I won't keep you long, and if you'd like, I can accompany you to your station and explain the delay."

"There's no need for that." She jerked her head toward the machines. "We're in plain sight of the entire room. There will be no question as to why I took longer than anticipated to return."

His stomach hollowed. Was he making fools of both of them? "Of course." He cleared his throat. "I *am* sorry about your father."

"You said that."

"What you said about not having any choice…are things that bad, uh, financially that you had to secure a job? Are Nadine, Tobias, and Heddie also here?"

Her cheeks pinked, and a sheen of moisture formed in her eyes, but she remained tense and unmoving. "I'd rather not discuss my personal situation with you, especially here, in the midst of prying ears, but I will tell you they're not working for the company."

"So—"

"So that's all you need to know. Now, I must really return to work. I don't want to be fired on my first day."

"I can help you. My parents—"

"We aren't interested in handouts. You do your job, and I'll do mine. And with any luck, we won't see each other very often." She pursed her lips. "Good day, Mr. Webber." She stalked away, head held high, looking neither right nor left as she strode to her machine.

Why was she so angry? Was she upset that he hadn't come by for a visit after returning home from college? Should he tell her he'd been in Chicago on business when the funeral occurred? Were her expectations such that they would renew their relationship, and she was offended because he hadn't made any overtures?

He huffed a breath and tugged at his collar. The letter he'd sent her during his sophomore year had explained everything. She had responded saying she understood, and that she wished him the best. He hadn't been home since then, working at various establishments over breaks to obtain experience. Why would she tell him that her situation wasn't his business? They'd known each other too long to stand on formalities or be embarrassed by unfortunate circumstances.

Shaking his head, he cast one last look at her, then shrugged and turned toward the door that would take him to the shipping department. His mouth dried as he caught sight of Mr. Beck standing on the threshold. How much had the man seen...or heard?

"Mr. Webber, a moment, if you please."

"Yes, sir." Ernst swallowed. The man's face was an iron mask, not the cordial visage he normally wore. "Your office or mine?"

"Mine."

Ernst cringed and nodded. He stuffed his hands into his front pockets as he walked beside the founder of the company...his boss's boss. Fortunately, noise from the various rooms they passed prevented the need or opportunity for conversation.

They arrived at the man's office and stepped inside. Large and well-appointed, but not opulent, the room overlooked the verdant plains of the surrounding countryside. Construction had not begun on this side of the company's property, so the land was still as pristine as when Ernst's parents had arrived decades ago.

Mr. Beck walked to the window and stared out the glass for a long moment. Ernst's heart thudded in his chest. What was going through the man's mind? He knew better than to ask.

"There seemed to be some sort of issue with the young lady to whom you were speaking." He moved away from the window, gestured for Ernst to take one of the vacant overstuffed chairs before lowering himself on the sofa. "I don't make it a practice to get involved in the daily operations of the factory. I have managers like you to handle that, but if I'm not mistaken, your interaction was about more than wrapping chocolate." Mr. Beck's gaze pinned him to the chair. "Am I right?"

"Yes, sir." Ernst rubbed the back of his neck. "We attended high school together. She is the daughter of one of the local farmers, and I didn't expect to see her."

"Because?"

"Her father was one of the men who opposed your purchasing the land and building the factory. He refused to consider being one of our milk providers."

Mr. Beck lifted one eyebrow. "What changed his mind?"

"Nothing. He has since passed away. I believe she may be here because of poor financial conditions. She loved working on the farm. I see no other reason for her presence. When I asked her about it, then offered my assistance, she became angry."

"Understandable. Most people don't want charity."

"But I want to help."

The man steepled his fingers. "She's more than a high school acquaintance, is she not?"

"We were sweethearts." Ernst plucked at the seam on his slacks. "But that was a long time ago."

"Perhaps not as long as you believe." Mr. Beck pursed his lips. "Mr. Webber, I make it a practice to stay out of the personal lives of my staff, but it appears that yours has made its way into my facility. Do you think your past with this woman will cause issues?"

Ernst bolted upright. "Not at all, sir. I can assure you I will have no problem maintaining a professional demeanor as will Miss Krause. She will be an excellent worker."

"For the moment, I'll take you at your word, but I will be watching. See that you keep your private life out of the office. Clear?"

"Crystal."

"Very good. You're dismissed."

Scrambling to his feet, Ernst stifled the desire to salute. Instead, he bowed, then walked to the door. He turned. "Thank you for your time, sir."

Mr. Beck gave him a curt nod, and Ernst slipped out of the office, perspiration dampening his hands and trickling between his shoulder blades. Could he maintain the promise he'd just made to the man?

Chapter Four

The cacophony in the wrapping room matched the rhythm of the throbbing in Ilsa's head. A week had passed, and she could almost operate her machine as fast as Zlata, but she was still struggling to get used to the noise. The girl had been gracious and patient while training her, never once criticizing or speaking harshly when Ilsa made a mistake. Bit by bit, they'd shared pieces of their lives, and she realized that as difficult as things were for her and her siblings, their situation couldn't compare to Zlata's experiences of famine and poverty, then the loss of her entire family before fleeing across Europe to make her way to America. Despite her friend's stoic face, Ilsa knew her heart bled.

A few others had also reached out to welcome Ilsa, inviting her to sit with them during breaks and regaling her with humorous incidents about their own beginnings at the company as they learned to operate the massive machines.

Break rooms were separated by gender, and she found she enjoyed not having to listen to loud and boisterous men while trying to relax. But mostly, she was glad she didn't have to worry about seeing Ernst. He'd made himself scarce since her first day, and a few surreptitious questions gave her the information about him she sought. He was a first-line supervisor like her own boss, Mr. Davison, but managed other sections of the factory. He was well-liked and respected, and more than a few girls commented about his good looks. She held her opinions to herself when that topic came up.

Rotating her neck, she massaged the stiffness from her shoulders. Factory work wasn't any harder than farm work, but standing in the same position hour after hour created cramps and tightness in her muscles. She'd have to toughen up if she planned to stay.

Who was she kidding? She had no choice but to keep her job. A smile broke out on her lips. On one hand, she didn't want to be here, but on the other, she'd proved she could do something other than farm chores, and do it well. And this afternoon on her way out, she'd receive her first week's pay. She'd already determined how to divvy up the money, and she couldn't wait to see the looks on her father's lenders when she handed them their payments.

She'd managed to create installment plans with every one of them. The discussions had been painful and embarrassing, but the men seemed to admire her for addressing the debt without flinching. It would be a long two years, but she'd make final reparations during the month of her twenty-sixth birthday. She twisted her lips. *Happy birthday to me.*

The bell rang, cutting through the dissonance. Machines were turned off, and the buzz of conversation replaced the metallic thumps and bumps.

Zlata walked over and gave Ilsa a one-armed hug. "You are doing so good. I'm proud of you. The last girl didn't work out. I thought it was my fault."

"You're a wonderful teacher." Ilsa smiled and picked up her lunch pail. "And your command of English is excellent."

"I read a lot. That is how I learned."

"What a great idea. I wouldn't have thought to do that." She followed the crowd to the break room. "But even with reading, I'm not sure I could learn Russian."

They entered the room and found seats at a nearby table. Yasmina glared at her from the far end. Ilsa dipped her head in acknowledgment, but refused to be intimidated or respond in kind.

Talking ceased as the women dug into their lunches, hunger taking precedence over socializing. Ilsa unwrapped her sandwich, thick slices of salty ham on bread Nadine had baked yesterday. Flavor exploded on her tongue as she chewed and thought about her siblings at home.

Nadine would be doing the laundry, theirs and that of the families she'd begun to take in. Tobias would be seeing to the animals as well as the crops. Should she have waited until after the harvest to apply at Beck's? Her brother labored from dawn to well past dusk for the past three days, coming into the kitchen to eat before tumbling into bed. Shadows hung below his eyes like half-moons.

Then there was Heddie. After marrying in a short ceremony, witnessed by her siblings and Billy's brother, she'd boarded the train and headed to Boston. Would love get her through the unknown? Would his family accept her? Did they feel about her German heritage how Ilsa had responded about his Irish background? Her face warmed. Who was she to judge? God saw no differences in people. She shouldn't either. *Oh, Mama, I could use your wisdom.*

"It's not fair the men are paid more than us." Yasmina's voice broke through Ilsa's reverie. "We work as hard as them. Why shouldn't we get the same salary?"

Several women murmured in agreement. Others were mute. Did that mean they didn't agree?

"But the men's jobs are more physically demanding. Don't you think that's worth something?" A blonde woman Ilsa hadn't met talked around a wad of food in her mouth. "Those sacks of cocoa beans must weigh fifty pounds. I wouldn't want to cart those around."

Yasmina stabbed her with a glare. "Big deal. So they have to tote around heavy stuff. Our jobs require more precision. That makes us just as valuable, if not more so."

The blonde shrank and dropped her gaze to her meal.

"Why don't they pay us all the same? Then they wouldn't have to figure out who's worth more." Magda Jasinski wiped her mouth with a cloth napkin. "All jobs are equally important. The company needs all of them."

"Yes, but would you want some new girl getting the same money as you?" Yasmina narrowed her eyes. "Let's say you've had the job for a year, and they hire someone with no experience. She shouldn't be paid the same."

Magda shrugged. "All right, so maybe they come up with a chart that pays by experience level."

"And who would make that chart? The managers who want to get paid a hefty salary?" Yasmina waved her fork. "No, the workers should decide."

A collective gasp went around the table, and Ilsa fixed her attention on her sandwich. Yasmina was alluding to unions. Had she already been approached by an organizer? Was she in charge of trying to get the employees rallied together to vote in the union?

Not everyone was happy that Mr. Beck had turned their sleepy village into a large town that was growing by the day. Houses and shops lined the once quiet streets, and the factory spread across acres that once held grazing cows. But many of the people who scraped a living out of the ground and depended on the weather now received regular paychecks. Tobias would say that was progress, but what at price had advancement come?

Mr. Beck seemed to care for his employees. He'd created a pleasant environment with amenities previously unavailable in their tiny hamlet. She'd grudgingly admitted to Nadine, just last night, she preferred being able to purchase ready-made clothes rather than hunch under the lamp sewing until her fingers cramped. She'd never been a good seamstress no matter how much her mother tried to guide her. Then after

Mama died, the act was too painful a memory. The playgrounds and schools made for happy, educated children. Highly skilled doctors manned the clinic Mr. Beck had opened.

She was beginning to disagree with her father's assessment of the owner. The price of development might be worth the changes in their lives. Did her opinion make her a bad daughter?

"What do you think, Ilsa?"

Her head jerked up. "What?"

Yasmina propped her elbows on the table and pursed her lips. "I asked what you thought about the topic at hand."

"You mean about pay?"

"Of course, that's what I meant. Haven't you been listening?"

"No. I've been thinking about something else."

"If you're going to be part of our group, you need to involve yourself in our issues." Yasmina's lips twisted. "Of course, if you think you're above us..."

"I've never held myself above anyone, no matter what you say." Ilsa laid down her sandwich and brushed crumbs from her palms. She raised her chin and met Yasmina's gaze. "I'm here to do a good job and receive my wages. I'm not looking to be part of some group. I want to work and then go home to be with my family."

"What little family you have left."

Ilsa's stomach coiled. "There's no call to be nasty, Yasmina."

"You can't not have an opinion. You need to take a stand."

"Says who?" Ilsa looked around the table. Some of the women seemed to watch the interchange as if it were a sporting event. Others studied their lunches, avoiding eye contact with their coworkers. Apparently, not everyone agreed with Yasmina.

"If you're not with us, you're against us."

"Hardly, but I see you'll badger me until I respond, so I will tell you that I've only been employed for a week. I'm grateful for my job and for the opportunity to earn a salary to help my family. I don't know how I feel about unions. That is what you're talking about, right? You've danced around the subject without actually saying the word. If you're so determined, perhaps you should be clearer with your protestations."

"Fine, yes, I'm talking about unionization. That's the only way we can get a fair shake." Yasmina poked out her lower lip, looking more like a toddler preparing for a tantrum than a young woman trying to make her point. "At some point, you will have choose, Ilsa. Make sure it's the right choice."

The bell clanged, announcing the end of lunch. As one, the women scrambled to their feet and headed out of the room. Ilsa stuffed her napkin into the pail, then huffed a sigh and trudged behind them. If Yasmina didn't like her before, she was sure to hate her now.

Zlata looped her arm through Ilsa's. "Don't give her another thought. She's been difficult since the day she started. She's an unhappy person and wants everyone else to suffer."

Ilsa nodded. "She's always been like this, even when we were girls in primary school."

"Not everyone wants the union."

"I could tell that by watching some of the others. They avoided looking at her. Everyone is entitled to their own opinion, but they are not required to share it."

"I agree." Zlata increased her pace. "We must hurry, or we'll be late for the bell that says we should be at our machines."

They entered the wrapping room, and Ilsa's shoulders fell. Ernst stood next to her station, an expectant expression on his face. Now, what?

Zlata squeezed her hand. "It seems Mr. Webber would like a word with you."

"Unfortunately, I think you're right." She nudged her friend's shoulder. "I'll tell you about it later."

"I can't wait." She winked and walked to machine.

Ilsa forced herself to relax. "How can I help you, Mr. Webber?"

"I've cleared it with your supervisor, but I need to speak with you for a moment."

"Certainly." She gestured to the far corner of the room away from prying ears. "Is over there sufficient?"

"Yes." They ambled to the spot, and Ernst turned to her. "I won't keep you long, but I wanted to make sure you're settling in all right."

She raised one eyebrow. "That's nice of you. I'm doing well. I'm nearly up to speed, and I enjoy most of my coworkers. I look forward to receiving my first check."

"About your coworkers, uh, there is some scuttlebutt floating around that some of the employees are thinking of inviting the union."

"Are you asking me or telling me?"

His faced reddened, and he licked his lips. "I wondered if you'd heard anything about it."

"Are you asking me to spy on my colleagues and report back to you?"

"Well, I wouldn't use the word 'spy.'"

"What word would you use?"

"Just listen to what they talk about during breaks, and let me know if their conversations revolve around unions."

"No. I won't do it, and it's unfair of you to ask. You're banking on our past friendship as a means to an end, and I don't appreciate it. I'm trying to make friends, not alienate people. Get one of those Pinkertons in here. Let them do your dirty work."

"Ilsa, please, this is important."

She pressed her lips together and shook her head. "Permission to return to work, Mr. Webber?"

"Mr. Webber? Ilsa—"

"Permiss—"

"Yes, go." He waved his hand, his mouth a thin line. "I won't bother you again."

She pivoted on her heel and marched to her station past Yasmina who gave her a knowing look. Wonderful, who knew what rumors she'd start. Why couldn't Ernst leave her alone? Was she wrong to turn down his request? Would she lose her job if she didn't cooperate? Why did life have to be so complicated?

Chapter Five

With a sigh, Ernst tugged down his sleeves, then brushed off unseen lint. Once again, he'd fouled things up with Ilsa. Thanks to college, he was book smart, but he still didn't know how to deal with women. Even one he'd known all his life.

Angry or calm, she was beautiful. Her blue eyes snapped with intelligence, and her porcelain skin shone with health despite the long hours standing in front of the machines. Some of the girls became sallow after weeks of employment, but he had a feeling Ilsa spent every spare moment outside. She'd always reveled in God's creation whether she was mucking the stalls, milking the cows, feeding the chickens, or working the land. She was a farm girl at heart.

Her expression had shown signs of fatigue, but not the worn-down appearance exhibited by some of the staff. Would she develop the look as time passed? Was the work too hard for her? She was a strong woman, having performed countless farm chores, but not masculine or overly muscular. Was her strength sufficient to do the job?

She'd changed since they'd parted. He had, so why was he surprised to see the difference in her? She didn't look older so much as more mature. Except when she was interacting with him, a smile always tugged at her lips, as if she held some joyous secret. Her stance was assured but not arrogant, her motions fluid and confident.

According to Mr. Davison, her supervisor, she'd caught on to the work immediately, making fewer mistakes than some of the women who'd been with the company since its inception. The man indicated she also showed more leadership capabilities than a few of the men. Female managers. Wouldn't that be something?

He reviewed their conversation and pinched the bridge of his nose. He'd asked her about her work, then jumped in with the request for her to perform reconnaissance among her coworkers. She probably thought he didn't care how she was doing, but had used the question as a way to set her at ease before asking the favor. Is that what he'd done?

Should he invite her to the house for dinner? His parents would be thrilled to see her again, but they might read more into the action than he meant. Would she? They'd been good friends, then more. Couldn't they be friends again? Was that an unrealistic expectation? If they became comrades, perhaps she'd change her mind about helping him find out about the union.

His chest tightened. She was too important to him to use her like that. And the last thing he needed was emotional entanglement, even as friends. He'd have to figure out another way to determine if the union was organizing. Would she share the information with Tobias? Would her brother be willing to tell him if she did?

Mr. Beck's words came to mind about whether or not Ernst could separate his personal and business relationships. How did one disconnect himself from others in a tiny village? Did he want to? If he was going to get ahead within the company, he needed to figure out how to do so. He scrubbed at his face with cold fingers. Life used to be much simpler.

"Something wrong, Webber?" Randall Rawlings, one of the other first-line supervisors, sauntered toward him, a smirk hovering on his lips. "Miss Krause get you down?"

"No, too much going on. That's all."

"Yeah, right." Randall wiggled his eyebrows. "Don't forget I know you two have a history. You hoping to reignite the flame? I don't blame you. She's one of the best lookers we have."

"That's enough, Randall." Ernst fisted his hands. "I'll not have you talk about her like that."

"Protective, aren't you? Yep, you're still in love with the gal. Although you shouldn't tie yourself down with just one of them. You're young, like me. We've got lots of time to pick one and get saddled with a family. I tell you, this is the best job on the planet."

"It's inappropriate to talk about the women's appearance, and my interest in Miss Krause is strictly professional. I hoped she had some information for me."

"Fine. You always were a stuffed shirt." The man huffed a breath. "What kind of information?"

"Nothing I'm willing to share at this time."

"Well, aren't you high and mighty?" Randall frowned. "I let you talk to her which will affect my production numbers, and you won't tell me what's up?"

"I'm not at liberty to say at this time." Ernst forced a smile. He wouldn't give the man a chance to spread gossip as he was known to do. "It's a project for Mr. Beck. I'll explain to him about your department's performance being my fault."

"Mr. Beck, huh?" The man puffed out his chest. "If you need help, let me know. I wouldn't mind the chance to show the old man what I'm capable of."

"Absolutely." Ernst clapped him on the back. "Thanks for understanding. I won't keep you any longer."

"No bother." Randall rocked back on his heels. "No bother at all."

Hurrying from the room, Ernst rolled his eyes. How had the man been hired? In the few classes they'd had together during high school, Randall had done poorly. Did he have some unknown skill that outweighed his lack of education and intellect? Nothing gave him the right to ogle the women or speak about them in a derogatory way. Ernst slipped into his office and closed the door. Should he alert Mr. Beck to the man's lascivious attitude or just keep an eye on him?

Looking through the glass that separated his office from the bean-sorting room, he studied his employees. The population reflected their village-turned-bustling-town. The largest percentage of workers were German. Most were the first generation of parents who'd fled their home country because of political or religious persecution. The next biggest group was the Swiss, many of whom had relatives in New Glaus. A huge community, they were on the forefront of the state's dairy movement nearly three decades ago. Cheese factories were popping up all over Wisconsin as a result.

The rest of his staff was made up of a few Italians and a smattering of Western and Eastern Europeans. They worked hard, made no problems, and were rarely tardy or absent. Did they think they were being treated unfairly? Did they want representation by the unions? He was back to his original conundrum. How would he find out about the union without alienating Ilsa?

Chapter Six

Humming, Ilsa opened the machine and fed the new stack of papers into the hopper. Two weeks had passed since Ernst asked her to spy on the other girls. He'd done as she asked and kept his distance, dipping his head in acknowledgment during the few times he passed through the department. She'd become accustomed to the noise, although she still missed the opportunity to spend most of each day outside. Despite the windows, which brought light into room, she missed fresh air and the warmth of sunshine on her back.

She closed the cover and fed a chocolate bar into the chute. She'd also grown used to the constant smell of chocolate, so much so, that she barely noticed it after an hour of arriving at work. She let her gaze bounce from the apparatus to the other girls, then back again. Most were friendly enough, but a few were standoffish or nasty. She avoided those as she was able, but breaks often forced them together.

Continuing to hum, she packed the bars into a box as they exited the machine. Grinning, she squared her shoulders. Mr. Davison told her yesterday that she was one of the best wrappers he'd ever had. As a result, he promoted her to a team leader which meant a little more money in her paycheck. She'd be able to pay off Papa's creditors sooner than planned.

A new girl would be starting tomorrow that she would train. She'd come far during the month since coming to work. From a nervous farm girl to someone who led a group of people and taught others how to do a job. She was beginning to understand Ernst's feelings about his career. Not that a job should be more important than people, but the satisfaction she had at the end of a day, knowing she'd been part of something big, was gratifying.

The company was still expanding. More people were moving to the area, creating congestion on the streets and in the shops. Mr. Beck had announced he'd be building more support structures to alleviate the crowds, but for now they'd have to make do. Fortunately, Nadine did most of the shopping during the day.

Movement at the far end of the room caught her eye, and she caught her lower lip between her teeth. Ernst strode into the room and gestured toward Mr. Davison. She hadn't seen Ernst in about a week. He looked good. Too good.

His charcoal-colored suit fit his across his broad shoulders and tapered at the waist. His shoes gleamed, and his shirt bright white and crisply ironed. Not one to wear pomade, his sandy-brown hair glistened in the harsh lights of the room. The two men stood close together as they spoke. His expression serious, Mr. Davison periodically glanced past Ernst at the workers. What could they be discussing that brought such a look to her supervisor's face? Her hand froze for a split second, then she continued her task. The union, of course.

"What's your boyfriend want with Mr. Davison?" Yasmina called from across the aisle. "This isn't his department. He should mind his own business."

Ilsa gritted her teeth and shrugged. She would not get pulled into an argument with the woman.

"It's bad enough you're getting favors from him. The least you can do is tell us what's up."

"I am not getting favors, and I have no idea what he's doing here. Leave me alone."

"Leave me alone," Yasmina spoke in a mocking tone. "You're lying. He's the reason you're a team leader. You shouldn't have gotten the job over others who have been here longer."

"I got the position because I do my job." She straightened her spine and lifted her chin. "And I don't make trouble."

"Says you."

"Look, if you don't like how things are going, quit or ask for a transfer."

"I was here first."

Zlata held up her hands as if in surrender. "Both of you go back to work. We're not supposed to talk."

"Sorry, Zlata." Ilsa's face warmed. "You're right." She bent her head over her machine and angled her body so she couldn't see Yasmina, but she could imagine the hateful look being cast at Zlata and her. No matter. She wasn't here to make friends.

Time passed, and the end-of-shift bell rang. The room swelled with conversations and laughter as the women headed toward the locker room. Ilsa picked up her lunch pail and followed them, her shoulders aching and a throbbing pain behind her left eye. She'd let Yasmina's nastiness get to her. *Father, help me see her through Your eyes.*

She tossed her jacket and cap into the large bin by the door, then plodded to her locker. She retrieved her pocketbook, coat, and wool hat. The weather had been unseasonably cold, and the bike ride to work been a chilly one. With the sun headed toward the horizon, the temperatures were sure to be frigid by now. She hadn't smelled snow in the air, but that could change quickly.

As she walked from the room, she slipped into her outerwear, tugging her hat over her ears. Outside, she went to her bike and tucked her purse in the basket hanging on the handlebar. A gust of wind whipped her coat around her legs, and she shivered. Winter appeared to be trying to come early this year. Did enough warm days remain to ripen the corn? A hard frost would damage the plants, and all of Tobias's work this season would be in vain. And they would lose the income they counted on.

Her chest tightened. *Please, God, keep our crops safe.* Another blast of air hit her, and she climbed onto the bicycle. Several pages of paper blew past, dancing and skipping on the wind. She dismounted and propped the two-wheeler against the rack, then ran after the papers and picked them up. As she stuffed the sheets under her pocketbook, she caught sight of a large headline:

GET WHAT IS RIGHTFULLY YOURS!!

UNITED WE BARGAIN...DIVIDED WE BEG

JOIN US!

10:00 AM SATURDAY, SEPTEMBER 25

FOUNDERS PARK

Ilsa pursed her lips and crumpled the pages. She shoved them into her pocketbook, got on her bike, and began to pedal. Did they see the irony of holding a union meeting in the park created by Mr. Beck? Or did they do it on purpose? Were they making a point?

As she approached the factory gates, the breeze tugged at her hat, and she hunched lower. She should have worn a scarf. Her face would be chapped by the time she rolled to a stop at home. Her mind raced as she cycled. Should she show Ernst the flyer? Had he already seen it? If he had been outside when the pages tumbled past, he'd have found out.

"Ilsa!"

She slowed and glanced behind her. Her pulse skittered. Ernst ran toward her. She would have to decide where her loyalties lay sooner than she'd planned.

##

Puffing slightly, Ernst drew alongside Ilsa. The fading sunlight cast shadows on her face as she cocked her head. Her expression was guarded, and her hands gripped the handlebar of her bike as if it were a lifeline. Tendrils of her ash-blonde hair stuck out from under her wool hat. Her bulky coat hid her trim figure.

"I must get home, Ernst. What do you need?"

He blinked. "I'm sorry to detain you, but I've been busy and didn't get a chance to come see you before now." He was babbling. She must think him a fool. "Ah, there is a special project, and you've been selected to take part. The work will start early next week, and I wanted to let you know as soon as possible."

Her eyes widened, and her lips parted. She studied him for a long moment. "Why me?"

"Because you've proven yourself adept at wrapping. One of the best and fastest. Your percentage of mistakes is low. We need someone with your accuracy."

"Why isn't Mr. Davison informing me if the project involves wrapping?"

"He's not in charge of the project. I am."

"You picked me?" She frowned. "I don't want favors or special treatment."

Ernst shook his head. "Actually, I had nothing to do with your being chosen. Mr. Beck asked your supervisor to recommend his best employee. He submitted your name. I had nothing to do with it."

Cheeks pink, her face brightened. "What does the job involve?"

Tension slipped from his shoulders, and he grinned. "Mr. Beck has produced a limited-edition chocolate in a three-dimensional triangle. Each piece must be hand-wrapped. We don't have a machine that can do the work. He's obtained a beautiful green foil to cover the chocolate and a tiny green box in which the piece will nestle. He's calling them indulgences."

"How many?"

"Initially, a thousand, but he's still collecting orders. He's approached his best customers with the opportunity to sell the item."

"I'll be taken off my regular machine? Department numbers will drop."

He cleared his throat. "Um, no. You'll be required to stay after hours. You'll work your full shift, then come to one of the large meeting rooms in the administration wing. You'll be paid for the additional time, of course. I hope staying late is all right with you."

"And if it's not?" She lifted one eyebrow. "Am I required to do this project?"

His heart fell. "Mr. Beck will go back to your supervisor and ask for another recommendation. You may say no." He spread his hands. "Listen, you took a job with us because you had to, so you're probably not looking for advancement, but participating in this sort of special assignment will look good in your employment record. Your willingness to go above and beyond will be considered as other positions become available."

"I'm not trying to be difficult. I just want to fully understand the company's expectations."

"So, you'll do it?" He held his breath. He hadn't told her the part about him working with her. He was being devious by withholding the information, but he pushed aside the guilt and waited for her answer. "You'd be great, you know."

She tapped her gloved index finger on her chin. "I take it you'll be my supervisor."

"Uh, yes." He should have known she'd figure that out. "Will working together be a problem, because if it is, I can see about other arrangements."

"You'd set aside your own opportunity to get me to take the assignment?"

"Yes. I agree with Mr. Davison. You're the best we have, and the project is important to the company, so you should be the one to do it."

"That's very unselfish, Ernst."

"I'm not a total boor."

"I—"

"Relax." He grinned, trying to put her at ease. They apparently still had a long way to go before their relationship was healed. "Will you do it?"

"Yes." A tentative smile curved her lips.

He whooped and pumped his fist. "Thank you! This is going to be great. The company will provide dinner after your regular shift, then we'll work on the project. I'll meet you in the hallway outside your department on Monday, so I can take you to the meeting room. After that, you can make your way there on your own."

Ilsa nodded. "Thank you for being so forthright, Ernst, about, well, everything."

He swallowed and laid his hand over hers on the handlebar. It was now or never. "Not entirely." Ernst licked his lips, then stuffed his hands into his front pockets. "I wanted to apologize for hurting you. You're angry with me—"

"I—"

"Let me finish. You're angry with me and have every right to be. I was callous about your feelings. We were in high school, and I cared for you as a boy does...in the moment, and with the excitement of new experiences at college, my affection faded. Stupidly, I thought my absence would affect you the same way, that you would move on to seeing others. I know now that I should have discussed the situation with you face-to-face. Instead, I hid behind a letter, then didn't come home during breaks, in order to avoid you. I'm sorry."

A sheen of moisture glistened in her eyes. She seemed to search his face, so he schooled his features, hoping that she could see that he genuinely regretted his actions. Despite the chill in the air, perspiration formed at his hairline as he waited for her response.

"I forgive you." Her face was terse. "Frankly, I don't want to, but we're both believers, and we're called to forgive others when we are wronged. I'm still angry and hurt, but with prayer, hopefully, I can set those aside." She narrowed her eyes. "Do you really think what we had in school wasn't real love? Just school crushes?"

"Don't you?"

"I asked you first, Ernst. I must know."

He bowed his shoulders. "To be honest, I don't know. I thought I loved you, but how could my feelings be so easily changed when we were apart?"

"Because you didn't know how good you had it." She smirked. "You let those college girls turn your head and lost the opportunity for something wonderful."

His throat thickened. "You're probably right. Can we start over...as friends? We were chums before we...it..." He rocked on his heels. "We had fun and enjoyed each other's company, even before high school."

"I'm not interested in spending time with you like friends do, but when we are together at work or see each other on occasion, I promise to be nice. No more snide comments. Is that acceptable?"

"Quite acceptable." He stepped back and motioned to the gate. "I'll let you go. It's getting late. Thank you for taking the job."

"Thanks for offering it." She gave him a curt nod, climbed onto the seat, and pedaled away.

His chest lightened. She'd forgiven him, albeit grudgingly, but he couldn't blame her for that. He didn't deserve her grace, but she'd bestowed it anyway, in her usual candid and plainspoken way. She'd never been one to mince words, and apparently, she hadn't changed in that regard. He grinned, and his heart quickened. Monday couldn't come soon enough.

Chapter Seven

The savory scent of fried chicken, mashed potatoes, and green beans pervaded the meeting room as Ilsa helped Ernst unpack the picnic he'd brought from home. The past two nights they'd dined on food from the employee cafeteria. Simple fare and not overly flavorful, but filling and warm. The meal his mother had created would rival the best restaurants in Green Bay, Milwaukee, or any other city in Wisconsin.

She poked several beans into her mouth and sighed as she chewed. Succulent and slightly sweet, they were cooked to perfection. Her bite of the potatoes had been creamy with a hint of butter and garlic. She could never have made anything this scrumptious. Like Mrs. Webber, Nadine and Heddie were gifted with the ability to cook whereas her skills definitely weren't found in the kitchen.

Silence blanketed them as they dined. She nibbled on a chicken leg, its crunchy coating contrasting with the juicy meat underneath. Her gaze wandered, and she took in the understated but attractive room. The walls were painted a muted green, and like other areas of the building, graced with artwork and other accoutrements. An eight-foot table stood in the middle of the room surrounded by Windsor chairs with padded seats that matched the wall color. A large urn of fresh flowers nestled in one corner. What sort of man spent his profits on flowers for his employees? Maybe he cared as much as Ernst claimed.

"You're awfully quiet tonight." His forehead wrinkled. "Are you too tired to stay?"

"No, just woolgathering." She put down the chicken and wiped her hands on a napkin, then pointed to the floral arrangement. "I was wondering about Mr. Beck. Why would he display such loveliness in a factory? That's money out of his pocket."

"He believes that a pleasant place to work creates happier employees, which makes them more productive. When I met him the first time, he shared with me how he visited other factories, in the States as well as overseas. Many were dark and foreboding. He said he was uncomfortable in them, so assumed the workers were, too. But there were two places he went to in England, and the facilities were well-lit with lots of windows. Like here, there were pictures on the walls, making the place seem almost homey. He could feel a difference in the employees when he toured."

"So, the flowers and other niceties are an investment."

He beamed at her. "Exactly."

Her pulse quickened at his admiration. Stop it, Ilsa. He's just being friendly. "No wonder Mr. Beck is successful. He's very savvy."

"I hope to learn a lot from him. I have already." He took a sip of coffee. "How are things going at the farm? I've been meaning to stop by to see Tobias."

"He misses Papa, but he seems to be enjoying the responsibilities and making the place his own. Papa was a bit set in his ways, and there are new processes and tools that are more efficient." A vision of her brother hunched over a catalog in front of the fireplace flitted through her mind. "We can't afford most of the equipment yet, but he's reading everything he can get his hands on. He's very smart."

"All the Krauses are." He winked at her. "Don't sell yourself short."

She shrugged. "Anyway, he was able to get an additional field planted with corn, and the crop seems to be doing well, so the harvest should be plentiful. He's considering adding other crops to diversify."

"I'm not surprised. Your brother is a born farmer." Ernst sipped his coffee. "He seemed embarrassed about not going to college after we graduated, but he would have been wasting his time there. His gift is with the land and animals. I have no doubt he will become highly successful. Whereas I can't tell the difference between wheat and rye."

"You have other skills." She giggled. "Like counting money and telling people what to do."

He chuckled. "Those are important." Leaning back in the chair, he laced his fingers behind his head. "What about you?"

"What about me?"

"Would you have stayed on the farm if you didn't have to find employment? During high school, you always talked about wanting to get away and do something different. I thought after graduation you might head to one of the cities."

"As the oldest, I had responsibilities." She fiddled with her napkin. "With Mama gone, Papa expected me to care for Tobias and the girls. Dreams of doing something other than farm work were unrealistic."

"That wasn't fair of him, you know." He pursed his lips. "You were young when she died. You needed raising yourself. You shouldn't have had to be a mother at that age."

"I resented him for a long time." Her voice was barely a whisper, and she ducked her head. She'd never told anyone how she felt, and saying it out loud seemed like a betrayal. She straightened and waved her hand. "Water under the bridge. If you're finished eating, we should get to work."

"We will." His tone was gentle. "It's obvious you want to change the subject, but I wanted to tell you how proud I am of you. You've had a difficult life, Ilsa, yet you're not bitter. You may have been angry at your father, but I never knew, and I have a feeling he never did either. You meet life head-on, with great faith and aplomb. I'm sorry you didn't get to realize your dreams, but perhaps after you and the others finish paying off the debt, you can revisit those aspirations and think about what you want."

"I'm afraid my faith is an illusion." She twisted her lips. "I question why God would take a mother and a father too soon."

"Questioning God doesn't mean you don't have faith. Some of the greatest men and women in the Bible railed against God. He wants our honesty. He can't help us if we're not truthful with Him. I wish I had an answer for you as to why He took your folks, but more learned men than me have been asking the same kinds of questions since the beginning of time."

Ilsa snorted a laugh. "Well, I've been very *honest* with Him." She climbed to her feet. "Enough philosophizing. There's work to be done, but first I should wash up rather than sending soiled dishes to your mother."

"I'll take care of it while you wrap."

"Fair enough. I'll be back shortly." She walked into the hallway, then made her way to the ladies' locker room where she could wash her hands and don a fresh jacket and head covering. Dinner had been lovely, almost like old times. They'd talked and laughed about everything and nothing. And he hadn't judged her for the resentment she'd felt against Papa. Rather he'd been compassionate, like he used to be.

Her pulse thrummed, and she glared at her face in the mirror's reflection over the sink. "Get a grip, Ilsa. He wants to be friends, nothing more. Besides, he's a college-educated executive. You are a lowly laborer. You no longer have anything in common. Stay until you can pay off Papa's debts, then leave."

She lifted her chin, dried her hands, and exited the room. It was going to be a long two years.

##

Ernst hummed under his breath as he carried the basket into the kitchen behind the employee cafeteria. He filled the sink, then shaved some soap chips into the hot water. He dunked the dinnerware into the suds and scrubbed them clean. After rinsing and drying the items, he laid them back into the woven container.

Doing the mindless chore was satisfying. Lately, he'd been in countless meetings and discussions as the management team planned the next phases of development within the company. He was pleased to be part of the process, evidence of his growing stature within the organization, but sometimes the endless talk was exhausting. Constant negotiating and posturing by everyone, himself included, drained him. Sometimes, at the end of a day, he felt as if he hadn't accomplished anything.

Working with Ilsa on the limited-edition chocolates invigorated him. He couldn't imagine bending over a machine day in and day out, but in the short term, the project gratified him in a way his management responsibilities didn't. She wrapped three indulgences for every one of his, and in the beginning, she'd had to correct him several times. However, his slowness was more because of the number of times he caught himself staring at her rather than his task.

She took pride in her work and seemed to enjoy the challenge of creating the special packages. He could see why Mr. Davison selected her.

He drained the water, wiped down the counters, and hung the dishrag over the spigot, then strode from the kitchen. An image of her face floated into his mind, and he quickened his pace back to the room. Intent on her task, she didn't look up when he entered, giving him the opportunity to drink in her beauty.

Dinner had been delightful. Tensions between them had eased, and the fact that she shared her feelings about her father made him think she'd lowered her guard and began to trust him again. He'd meant what he told her. He was proud of her. Other than his mother, Ilsa was the strongest woman he knew, and not just physically. Sure, she'd pulled her weight, sometimes literally, on the farm, but she'd practically raised her siblings when her father abdicated responsibility during his grief. While keeping the household running, she taught all three of them how to be God-fearing, productive adults.

Setting down the basket, he approached the table as she raised her gaze to his. He put two fingers to his forehead in a mock salute. "Ready to work, ma'am."

Her eyes sparkled, and she jerked her head to a towering stack of wrapped chocolates. "It's about time you returned."

He gaped at the pile, then shook his head and grabbed an empty box. "You're amazing. Almost as fast as a machine."

Face pink, she lifted one shoulder in a delicate shrug. "I doubt that, but thank you for the compliment."

Packing the carton, he glanced at her. "You know lots of colleges accept women now."

"Uh-huh." She continued to wrap without looking his way.

"What area of study would you choose?"

At that she jerked up her head and pursed her lips. "Who said I want to go to college? Would you be disappointed if I said I wasn't interested?"

"Not disappointed, but surprised. As I said, you're highly intelligent. You could get a degree in any field you choose."

"But could I get a job in that field?" Her gaze dropped to her work. "You know as well as I do, the options for women are limited. Things have changed, but not enough. I can be a team leader but not a supervisor, a nurse but not a doctor, a teacher but not a principal. And frankly, it's worse here in little-old Cocoaville. Why get a degree when I can only advance part of the way?"

Ernst scratched his jaw. "I feel like I have to apologize on behalf of all men."

"Don't be silly." She shot him a quick smile. "There are plenty of women who think we should remain in the home raising children or leave certain jobs to men."

"If there were no barriers whatsoever, what would you choose?"

"Seriously?"

"Seriously." He propped his chin on his hand. Why had he never asked her that before? "I want to know."

She sat back and crossed her arms. "Art. I love sketching and painting." Her face glowed as she spoke. "Mostly watercolors, but oils, too. Putting God's creation onto paper brings me great joy, and I'd love to share that with others." Her smile faltered. "But it's not practical. Papa and Mama both said that."

"I remember some of the pieces you did when we would picnic or sit by the river. You're very talented. There are plenty of artists who make a living with their work."

"Name three."

"I backed myself into that, didn't I? But I'm at a loss. Art isn't exactly my forte." He gestured to one of the landscapes on the wall. "I couldn't tell you who painted that."

With a snicker, Ilsa rolled her eyes. "Guess that fancy degree isn't worth as much as you think."

Throwing back his head, Ernst guffawed. "Point taken. But I still think you should consider pursuing something that you love after you've left Beck's."

"Are you trying to get rid of me?" she joked.

"Of course not, but you made it plain from the beginning that working here isn't your lifelong plan."

"True." Her eyes took on a distant haze. "It would be wonderful to go to art school, then create beautiful pictures, but I need to keep my head out of the clouds. That takes money and time, neither of which I have in abundance." She bestowed a dazzling smile on him. "But thank you for asking."

His heart sped up. "I should have asked a long time ago. Do you still draw? Do you have pieces you could show me? I'd love to see your work." He snapped his fingers. "In fact, we should show Mr. Beck, and maybe he would hang some of it. We could ask other employees if they have artwork they'd like to display. Paintings, sculptures, and woodcuts. Wouldn't that be wonderful?"

"For others, perhaps, but not for me. I'm not ready to share my handiwork with the public." She reached for another stack of foil. "Your idea has merit, but you should consider how to manage submissions. Would everything be accepted? If not, you don't want a disgruntled employee because you didn't like his or her art."

He slapped his forehead. "Good point. Perhaps I'll bury that brainchild."

"Not for long. I like the concept, but it needs to be planned out and explained. If people know going in that their items might not get chosen, they might not feel as badly if that happened. Or perhaps you do accept everything. Do you want perfection or a representation of your employees?"

"You've given me a lot to think about, Ilsa." He closed the lid on the full box. "I'm sorry about your financial situation, and the fact you didn't get to do what you wanted, but I'm glad you're here." More than he could say.

Chapter Eight

Before Ilsa could respond, Ernst picked up the box and carried it down the hall to the storage closet where Mr. Beck was staging the order. Would she read meaning into his words? He nibbled on his lower lip. What was he getting himself into? Mr. Beck's statement pushed its way into his mind. Could he separate his personal and business lives? His head said yes, but his heart seemed to be in disagreement.

His pulse raced when he caught sight of her, and his brain seemed to be made of cotton candy when he had to speak with her, alternately being rendered speechless and blurting out things that should remain inside.

Shifting the carton to one hand, he unlocked the door, then tucked the box into the dim recesses of the cupboard. He secured the door, then turned and made his way back to the meeting room where she was diligently wrapping the chocolates. Mr. Beck had picked up three more orders, so the initial count of one thousand had tripled. He'd gasped at the news, but Ilsa seemed undaunted when he told her.

She'd already finished several dozen in the time he'd been gone. He retrieved another empty box and began to fill it. When he'd caught up, he reached for a stack of foil and began to wrap. His fingers fumbled with the fine metallic paper, and he forced himself not to rush, but his attempts were poor at best. He huffed a sigh, pushed aside the flimsy material, and returned to filling the box.

"Not everyone is cut out to be a wrapper." She gave him a saucy smile. "We've already talked about what your gifts are."

"Funny. Yes, we did." He shrugged. "You know you don't have to work so quickly. We're making good time with the project."

"Why would you want me to slow down? The longer I work, the more you have to pay me."

"Is that a problem?"

"Are you giving me charity again?" Her mouth thinned. "We also talked about that."

He held up his hands. "That's not what I'm doing. You're working long hours. Your brother could talk to you about pacing yourself. Eventually, you wear yourself out if you work flat out. You're no good to us if you overtire yourself."

Her expression eased. "That makes sense. I'll give you that one."

"Whew." He made an exaggerated motion of running his hand across his forehead. "I wouldn't be doing my job as your manager if I didn't take care of you. That's another one of Mr. Beck's philosophies, and I like it."

"Me, too." She stopped wrapping and rotated her neck, then massaged her shoulders. "During the day I get caught up in moving as fast as I can. We girls feel like that's what Mr. Davison expects. I don't know if it's the case, but that's our perception."

Ernst stilled. He shouldn't get involved in another manager's department, but he'd like to know if the man was working his girls too hard. Production numbers were important, but so was employee health. Another of Mr. Beck's sayings.

"If I wasn't so bad at wrapping, I'd help." He pointed to several pieces of mangled foil. "But as we've determined, packing is more my style."

"And you're doing a fine job."

"Thanks for the encouragement," he said drily. "But in all seriousness, this project has gotten me thinking about gifts and talents."

"In what way?" Her hands never stopped moving as she spoke.

"Take the wrapping department as an example. The entire staff is women. Why is that? Are they better suited to the task than men? Do smaller hands make for better wrappers?"

"The gals operate machines. Surely, the men could do that just as easily." She stacked a completed chocolate and started on another. "If some of the girls are to be believed, the job pays less than some of the others. Perhaps men don't take it for that reason. Or does the company only interview women for that position?"

"Hmm. I'm not sure. I'll have to look into that." He packed the finished pieces. "Then to your way of thinking, men and women can receive the same sort of gifts or talents from God."

"Are you referring to gifts of the spirit as in the Bible? That requires further study. I know He says things specifically about men and women, but I haven't studied those passages at length. But as far as talent goes, like whether someone is mechanically inclined, I don't think God differentiates."

"A man could be a good cook, and a woman could be adept at building houses."

"Exactly!" She looked pleased, then snickered. "Although, I wouldn't do well at either one of those."

"But you do an excellent job at detailed work, like wrapping these special chocolates. And I've seen your needlework. You have an excellent hand."

"And eating. I manage a knife and fork rather well, if I do say so myself."

"Yes, you do. I'm not too bad at that either." He laughed. "But I'm definitely better at tasks like taking out the trash, shoveling, and—"

"Talking. You're very good at talking."

"That's what makes me a good manager."

"Uh-huh." She sighed and stretched her arms over her head. "Unless you're hiding another batch of indulgences, I'm finished for the night." She rubbed her eyes, then climbed to her feet. "Let me help you pack them."

"Nope, that's my job. You drop off your jacket and cap, then grab your personal things, and I'll meet you at the back door to take you home."

Her cheeks pinked. "It's not that far. I can ride my bike."

He pulled out his pocket watch. "It's nearly nine o'clock, too dark for you to cycle. If it makes you feel better, I'm headed that way. I need to deliver something to the Ushers. I promised them I'd leave it on the porch tonight." He waved his hands. "Get along. I'll be there shortly."

"If you insist."

"I do."

"All right. Thank you." She slipped from the room, her footsteps fading.

With quick motions, he put the remaining chocolates into a carton, then took several trips to carry the filled boxes to the storage area. He wiped down the table, pushed in the chairs, then turned off the light and headed out.

Thankful she was allowing him to drive her home, he increased his pace. He relished the time with her. The hours were long, but he felt refreshed at the end of each shift, and she was the reason. Their conversations were rich and varied: sometimes serious like tonight and sometimes fanciful like the night they'd discussed their favorite desserts.

Her intelligence made him dig deep to respond to her comments and questions. He looked forward to delving into the Bible to learn what the Book said about gifts, then discussing what he'd found. He stopped in his tracks. Since when did he want to study God's Word? Raking his fingers through his hair, he began to walk again. Ilsa had done it again. Like in high school, she'd burrowed her way into his heart and mind. But the feelings that sent his pulse skipping were nothing like they'd been then.

Chapter Nine

The bell rang, and Ilsa blew out a loud sigh. Finally at an end, the day had dragged like molasses in January. Her entire body ached, and her eyes burned. Unless Mr. Beck had obtained additional orders, she should be able to finish the special project this evening. The extra money in her paycheck was a blessing, but she looked forward to tomorrow when she could go home after work and put up her feet.

Conversation ebbed and flowed around her as she made her way to the locker room to retrieve her pocketbook and lunch pail. Laughter punctuated the air, and she smiled. The women were in a festive mood today.

As she trudged down the corridor, she glanced out the window, and the tension slipped from her shoulders. The trees seemed to be lit from within, their fiery red, tangerine orange, and golden yellow leaves appearing like a blaze against the lush green meadows. Late afternoon sun glowed in the dusky-blue sky. How she missed spending the bulk of her day outside.

With a last glance at the beauty, she entered the locker room. Being in the factory was a means to an end. She didn't have to work here forever, just long enough to pay off their creditors. She tamped down the surge of anger at Papa for leaving them in such dire straits. He'd had his reasons for what he did. Who was she to judge? And as he used to say, "Hard work never hurt anyone." She twisted her lips. Tell that to her screaming muscles.

She threaded her way through the giggling women in various states of disarray. Their chatter was reminiscent of the clucking in the henhouse on the farm. What would they think if they knew?

A group of women surrounded Yasmina, who looked at her with an ugly sneer, then dropped her gaze. As Ilsa reached her locker, the girls stopped talking, their silence saying more than their words. She hadn't understood Yasmina's dislike during high school, and she couldn't figure out why it continued. She'd done nothing to the woman, then or now. But apparently some perceived slight or misdeed had set her against Ilsa from the beginning. It had to be exhausting to hold on to hatred for so long.

She unlocked the latch, then opened the door to the cabinet, and reached inside. A fine coating of cocoa powder covered her coat, hat, pocketbook, and lunch pail. She gritted her teeth, but held her tongue. She wouldn't give whoever did this the satisfaction of seeing her get upset. Schooling her features, she pulled out the items, slung them over her arm, and turned to leave.

"I don't understand people who think they're better than everyone." Yasmina's voice cut through the hubbub in the room. "I mean, we're all the same here."

"Well, some people get special favors," one of her friends piped up as she blocked Ilsa's path. "They get treated differently, so that makes them think they're important."

Lifting her chin, Ilsa looked down her nose at the woman. "Please let me through."

"Sure." The woman sneered but didn't move. "You don't want to be late for your *meeting*."

"I asked nicely. Please move."

"I asked nicely. Please move," Yasmina mimicked Ilsa in a squeaky voice, then rolled her eyes. "What some people will do to get ahead astounds me."

"If I *meet* with the boss, do you think I'll get a cushy assignment?" Yasmina's cohort crossed her arms and glared at Ilsa. "I'm more his type than you are."

Ilsa's cheeks heated. "How dare—"

A firm hand on her arm yanked her through the women. "Don't say another word. They'll only figure out a way to use it against you."

"Nadia?"

"Yes." Nadia Latkowski was one of the newer employees in the wrapping department. Petite and dark-haired, she rarely spoke. They made their way out of the locker room, and Nadia pulled her close to the wall, then released her, her face pink. "I've been subjected to their taunts. You will lose if you engage them. I know this."

"But they think Ernst and I are doing something wrong. I have to correct their assumptions."

"You will never change them." Nadia shook her head. "I am new here, and perhaps have no right to talk to you like this, but I was afraid you would get in trouble. Somehow Yasmina or one of her girls will make the argument seem like your fault."

"You're right." Ilsa sagged. "I had to deal with her in school. She got more than a few students in trouble with her lies." She held up her coat. "But she's now stooping to vandalism, and I don't appreciate it. If one of the managers sees this..."

"They will be upset at the waste and might think you are stealing product."

"Exactly."

Nadia jerked her head toward the bathroom. "You go in there and clean your things. I will inform Mr. Webber that you were, uh, held up and will arrive shortly."

"There's no need for that. He knows I'll be there when I'm able." She smiled. "I'd rather have your assistance with this mess."

"Absolutely."

They went inside the lavatory, and Nadia grabbed a pair of towels from the pile on the shelf. She dampened them. "You hold up your garment, and I will brush off the chocolate."

"How about if I shake the garment first."

Nadia snickered. "Then we'll have to clean the entire floor and possibly ourselves."

"Of course. I hadn't thought of that."

"Before coming here, I worked as a laundress. I can get anything clean." She rubbed the towel in downward strokes, and the powder fluttered to the ground in a small pile. "See?"

"Yes, thank you." Ilsa cleared her throat. "Yasmina had been mean to you, too. You should talk to Mr. Davison. We can't let her get away with her behavior."

"If thine enemy is hungry, give him bread to eat. If he be thirsty, give him water to drink. For thou shalt heap coals of fire upon his head, and the Lord shall reward thee." Nadia shrugged. "I am to live above reproach. If I stoop to her methods, she will never know the love of God."

Ilsa gaped at her. "You're a believer?"

"Yes, but not according to some of the girls."

"I don't understand."

Nadia bent and wiped up the chocolate dust, then balled up the towel and put it in the canvas bin. "I am Catholic. The Protestants think my beliefs are wrong, so they make fun of me."

"That's terrible." Ilsa's eyes widened. "They have no right to do that."

"Catholics have been persecuted for many years in countries around the world. We are used to it. That is why I know that you can never change people. They will think what they will, but the Lord calls me to be nice to her, so I bite my tongue.”

“You shouldn’t have to get used to it.”

“My parents hoped when they came to America, life would be different.” She spread out her hands. “We are blessed with money and food, but friends...”

Ilsa grabbed her hands and gave them a quick squeeze. “I will be your friend. I am also a believer, and we will focus on the similarity that we love the same God. How does that sound?”

“Lovely.” Nadia beamed. “Now, you must go. Mr. Webber has waited long enough, and those candies won’t wrap themselves.”

“Nothing is going on between us,” Ilsa blurted. “We were...friends. Well, more than friends, in high school.”

“You don’t owe me an explanation, but I have watched you and know that you are filled with integrity. You are an honest woman.” She nudged Ilsa’s shoulder. “I will not ask, but it might be difficult for you to work with him because of your past. I will pray for you.”

“That means a lot to me. Sometimes it is hard, but I’m getting more used to seeing him. We could never...you know... We’re too different now.” She grabbed a towel, wiped down her purse and lunch pail, then tossed the fabric into the bin. “Anyway, I must go. Thank you...friend.” Nothing could come of a relationship with Ernst, but her pulse refused to obey her as it sped up on her way down the corridor to the meeting room.

Ernst hesitated outside Mr. Beck's office and tugged on his sleeves. He smoothed his jacket, then checked himself for stray threads or lint. Satisfied he was presentable, he knocked. The founder's deep voice rumbled, bidding him to enter. With a deep breath, Ernst swung open the door, then stepped inside. "You wanted to see me, sir?"

Hunched over a thick stack of papers, the man looked at him over his wire-rimmed spectacles and gestured toward a vacant chair near the desk. "Yes. Make yourself comfortable. I'll be a few moments."

"Yes, sir." Ernst sat and laced his fingers while he surveyed his surroundings. The man's office never ceased to impress him. Well-appointed, but not opulent, the room appeared more like a study one might find in a home than the suite of a wealthy business owner. The bookcases and desk were constructed of maple rather than mahogany, and the upholstery on the chairs was good quality, but not silk or satin. Like other parts of the factory, artwork hung on the walls: landscapes, with the exception of a gilt-framed oil painting of Mr. Beck's wife.

The man had been a confirmed bachelor until he met Mrs. Beck during a business trip to Boston. Daughter of a merchant, she worked in a ladies' dress shop that Mr. Beck had visited in order to purchase a birthday gift for his mother. Within six months, they were married, and a year later he'd sold his caramel business to begin his foray into chocolate. Rumor had it he discussed every decision with her. She periodically came to the factory, but Ernst met her the first time in their home when he'd been asked to deliver an urgent missive.

Petite to the point of appearing childlike, Mrs. Beck held a regal bearing. She'd been wearing an emerald-green dress, and her blonde hair piled high on her head, giving her additional height. Bright with intelligence, her eyes were pewter gray, set deep over porcelain-like cheeks. She'd taken the letter, then congratulated him on obtaining a job with the company, smiling as if she were his own mother, proud of his accomplishments. She'd insisted he stop by the kitchen for something to eat before he left, then glided from the room.

The portrait was lifelike, the artist having captured her features perfectly. One corner of her mouth tilted up, and her expression made him think she harbored a delightful secret. She was posed in front of a stone fireplace, the couple's Boston Terrier sitting at her feet. He'd heard the dog bark somewhere in the house during his visit, but had not met the pup.

"Beautiful, isn't she?"

Ernst's head whipped around, his face scorching. What must the man think of him staring at his wife? "Yes, sir. I was recalling the first time we met. Your wife is a gracious hostess."

"I am blessed to have found her. She is the perfect partner." Mr. Beck took off his glasses and laid them on the desk. "Perhaps you will be as lucky."

"I'm in no hurry to marry, sir."

"Neither was I, then I met Mrs. Beck." After a last glance at his wife's image, he leaned back in the chair. "The love of the right woman will change your mind. And speaking of women, I wanted to compliment you on your choice of using Miss Krause for the special project. She has done a commendable job. Her work is flawless, and she finished before the deadline."

"Thank you, sir, but if you'll recall, Mr. Davison is the one who initially recommended her."

"But you made the final decision." He scribbled something on a notepad, then crossed his arms. "I'm giving both of you a bonus that will appear in your next paycheck. Be sure to inform her ahead of time."

Ernst straightened. "Yes, sir, and thank you. You're very generous."

"Tut. No less than you both deserve." Mr. Beck waved in a dismissive motion, then rubbed his palms together. "What can you tell me about the unions? Have you learned anything yet?"

"Nothing concrete." Ernst ducked his head. "I, um, quizzed Miss Krause about the situation, but she didn't know anything."

Mr. Beck chuckled. "Your tone says she wasn't happy at being asked."

"Said she wouldn't spy for me. Not that I asked her to."

"Of course not. None of the unions are keen on letting in the women, so she may not be privy to any information. However, I did hear a rumor that the gals are considering starting their own association."

"Really? Can they do that?"

"As long as they file the appropriate paperwork, I would think so, but I'm disappointed that anyone wants the unions here. I've done my best to ensure employees are well-paid and provided for. They can rent or own their homes, lovely homes, and pay is more than equitable. We have shops, doctors, hospitals, and schools. They should do their homework and compare their lives with those who work for some of the railroad barons."

"The newspapers have naught but negativity about one in particular."

Mr. Beck gave him a noncommittal grunt, then cocked his head. "Is there anyone else who might be willing to share information...not spy, but if he or she hears something, would come forward with it?"

Tobias's image came into Ernst's mind. "I'm not sure."

"Care to elaborate?" Mr. Beck lifted one eyebrow. "Your intuition hasn't proven you wrong yet."

"I'm, or at least was, friends with Miss Krause's brother, Tobias."

"The name isn't familiar. Is he one of ours?"

"No, he works the family farm, but I can try to renew our relationship. I haven't seen him but a couple of times since my return to town. He may be buddies with some of our employees."

"Excellent. Take your time. We don't want to spook him."

"Yes, sir." Ernst swallowed. But would his plan spook Ilsa?

Chapter Ten

Ilsa eyed the purple and pink streaks in the sky as she pedaled down the dirt lane toward the house. A brand-new week and the third day since she'd finished the special project meant she could get home before dark. An unseasonable warm breeze stroked her cheeks and ruffled her hair. She braked the bicycle and dismounted while surveying the property.

Not too much longer and the crops would be ready for harvest. As far as she could see, cornstalks oscillated in the wind, their green shafts swaying like a troupe of lithe ballerinas. The lush meadows were vacant. Tobias must have finished putting the cows in the barn for the night. If he was still there, he would probably appreciate some help.

She walked her bike toward the large building, the musky smell of hay, animals, and manure ripening the air as she approached. Snuffling and lowing greeted her, and she leaned her cycle against the doorway. She'd put it on the porch after finishing with her brother.

"I'm sorry about your papa, Tobias." Ernst's warm tones wafted out of the opening. "He was a good man."

Freezing in place, Ilsa strained to see into the dim recesses of the building. Ernst's horse must be inside, or she would have been alerted to his presence. Why was he here?

"Thank you. We miss him."

"How are you adjusting? Is there anything my parents or me can do to assist?"

"We're doing as well as can be expected and are managing." Tobias's voice was tight. "The fields are nearly ready for harvest, and it seems like it will be a good one. Changing over to corn has proved to be a good decision."

"Will you be able to pull in the crops on your own? Surely, you'll need more people."

"Yes, but I've made arrangements with the farmers who abut our property. In addition to our cows, we all have some levels of yield that need to be brought in. We've worked out a rotating scheduling to work together."

"That's brilliant." Admiration colored Ernst's words. "Must have been your idea."

Silence. Tobias must have shrugged or gestured his response.

Ernst continued, "I should have visited sooner, Tobias. I hope you'll forgive the lapse."

"Nothing to forgive, my friend. Moving home and a new job kept you busy, I'm sure. Your parents must be thrilled to have you."

"They are. Mother is doing her best to make up for the time I was gone. Preparing all my favorite foods, and that sort of thing."

"I'll speak to Nadine about having your folks over for dinner. It would be nice to catch up with them."

"We wouldn't want to intrude."

"Nonsense." Tobias sighed. "They came to Papa's funeral, and we spoke then about doing so, but nothing came of the conversation. Your parents always treated us like their own children. I miss seeing them."

"Then we will make it a habit to get together. Now, are you sure there isn't something I can do to help?" Ernst cleared his throat. "I know about your, uh, financial situation, from talking with Ilsa."

"She told you?"

"Reluctantly, but yes. I'm glad you will have a successful harvest in addition to her salary, but are they enough? I don't want to pry, but I would hate to see you lose the farm."

A deep sigh sounded, and Ilsa leaned forward, pushing away her guilt at eavesdropping.

"We have payment plans with all of our creditors, and we have to live carefully, but I believe we will come out all right in the end. I pray nothing breaks."

"I may have a solution for you."

"I'm listening."

"The company is growing exponentially. Mr. Beck seems to have struck gold with his chocolate because we are getting orders from all over the country. He continues to develop new products and recently came up with a limited-edition item that may end up in our full line."

"Congratulations. As you know, Papa hated Mr. Beck for coming in with his factory. Said he was a traitor to his heritage, as a farmer and a German."

"And how do you feel?"

"Growth is a good thing, whether in a farm or a factory. If a business isn't moving forward, it is stagnating. And Mr. Beck has proven himself to be a benevolent employer and good neighbor. His success has overflowed into the community. Many people are no longer living hand to mouth, us included. Having a contract to supply milk to you has benefited us greatly."

"We are hiring faster than we are able to build housing for our new employees, so we are looking for people who would be willing to take in boarders, some temporarily, others on a long-term basis. Would you be interested?"

Clapping one hand over her mouth to smother a gasp, Ilsa stifled the desire to run inside to be involved in the conversation. Would Tobias make the decision for them?

"Potentially." Tobias snickered. "But far be it for me to make a decision without consulting with the girls. Nadine would have my head if I agreed to this without her. It adds more work to her already full plate. And I don't know if Ilsa would want to work all day at Beck's, then come home to live with coworkers."

"I see your point."

"How much time do I have to decide?"

"The sooner the better, because I'd like to give you the managers."

"That would make for better cash flow."

"Exactly."

"Isn't your giving us first choice showing favoritism, Ernst?"

"Perhaps, but I know your family would provide an excellent experience, the kind Mr. Beck wants for his senior staff. Nadine is a great cook, and your farm is a beautiful and serene setting, one that would be relaxing for these men after a long day at the office."

"Fair enough. I'll discuss this with them tonight. In fact, you could join us, then you would be able answer their questions."

"No, I've got appointments with three other families to discuss becoming a boardinghouse."

"Too bad. I happen to know Nadine has made *Rouladen* and *Kartoffelknödel.*"

"You're killing me. I love her potato dumplings, and I haven't had beef rolls in years."

"You could be late..."

"Tempting, but no."

"Thank you for coming by, Ernst. I'm glad you're home. I'm not a letter writer, and I've missed talking with you."

"I'm happy to be here, too. We will have many more good times to come. Your being a first-rate farmer is a mixed blessing. You provide us with milk, but I'd much rather see you in the factory. Your mechanical capabilities would be of great service to us."

"Factories are the wave of the future, with their machinery and modernization, and it would be exciting to work for your Mr. Beck, but I'm needed here. Nadine and Ilsa couldn't have handled the amount of manual labor required on the farm. It made more sense for one of the girls to be with you."

"Do I want to know how you all determined who would work at Beck's? Did Ilsa lose or win?"

"Funny, Ernst. We were quite logical about the decision. We discussed skills and abilities, and she is the best fit for Mr. Beck. Her selection for a special project indicates we were right."

A scream pierced the air. Ilsa whirled and raced to the house. She hurried up the steps and shoved open the door. Smoke poured down the hallway. "Nadine? Where are you?"

"In the kitchen."

As Ilsa hurried into the kitchen, the gray cloud enveloped her. She waved her hand to dispel the haze as footsteps pounded behind her. Ernst and Tobias had heard the shriek, too. Coughing, she put the inside of her elbow against her face. "What—"

A lantern lay in pieces on the floor, and a blaze licked the wall and curtains where the oil had spattered. Nadine wrestled with her skirt which was on fire, the flames climbing toward her waist. "Nadine—"

Ernst shouted, "Tobias, you and Ilsa see what you can do about the house. I've got Nadine." He grabbed her towel, pushed her to the floor, then rolled her over. "Cover your face, Nadine." He continued to turn her back and forth.

An empty pail sat by the sink, and Ilsa snatched it up. *Thank You, Father, for providing the means to put out the fire.* She pumped water into the bucket, then handed it to Tobias who tossed its contents on the burning fabric. She filled a pitcher, then the bucket again, pulling and filling vessels she yanked from the shelves. Her brother ripped down the curtains and stomped them with his boots. *Please let Nadine be unharmed.*

The fire was soon out and the flames on Nadine's clothes extinguished. Smog shrouded the room, and Tobias opened the door. Fresh air swept through the room, and the cloud dissipated. Ilsa sighed and wiped the perspiration from her forehead with the back of her hand.

Her sister cried quietly, and Ernst helped her into a chair. "Are you burned anywhere, Nadine?"

"No. I'm so embarrassed."

Ilsa squatted next to her, aware of Ernst's proximity on her sister's other side. "Accidents happen. I'm just glad we were here to take care of it. What happened?"

"The wick was too high, and I tried to adjust the level while the lamp was in my hand. I fumbled with the chimney and dropped everything. Stupid of me."

"Like Ilsa said, accidents happen. We're glad you're all right."

Tobias handed Nadine a glass of water, and she gulped the liquid. Finishing, she pushed them away and rose. Her cheeks blazed. "I must change my clothes, then clean up this mess."

"Nadine—"

"I'll be back shortly." She strode from the room

Exchanging a glance with Ernst, Ilsa shrugged, then collected the empty pitchers, bowls, and bucket and piled them into the sink. Tears pricked the backs of her eyes. If he hadn't been here, would they have been able to save Nadine? "How did you know what to do to put out the flames on Nadine's clothes? I would have tried to strip them off or throw water on her."

"Part of the training we receive as managers includes fire safety. Mr. Beck had a fire chief come speak with us, and he showed us several techniques. That was one of them. Perhaps the company should hold a session for employees. As we saw, this knowledge is important in the home, too."

His gaze seemed to caress her face, and her pulse thrummed. Would she never get over this man?

Chapter Eleven

The machines clattered around her as Ilsa flexed her fingers, then massaged her neck muscles. Her forehead throbbed, and her eyes felt as if lint was caught under her lids. She'd been loath to come to work today, but Nadine insisted she was fine and wanted no help in setting the kitchen to rights. Tobias would be there, but this was the first time Ilsa had been separated from them during a time of need. It had always been the four of them, and they'd drawn closer after Papa's death, even with Heddie far away. They corresponded frequently with her, so it was almost as if she were still home.

A sigh slipped from Ilsa's lips, and she turned her wayward attention back to her apparatus. Moping wouldn't do anyone any good, especially if she didn't meet her quota. She raised a quick gaze to Zlata across the aisle. The girl caught her glance and grinned as her hands flew through her task. Ilsa returned her smile, her dark mood lifting. She had her family, her faith, her health, and her friends. The damage to the house was minimal and easily repaired. She had no reason to be morose. *Forgive me, Lord.*

She checked the hopper. Nearly out of wrap. She shut off the machine, then strode to the far end of the room where she retrieved a supply of foil. Cradling the pile in her arms, she made her way back and filled the machine. The walk had blown the remaining cobwebs from her mind, and she began humming "Amazing Grace," her favorite hymn. Her spirit lifted further. God was good. That was all she needed to focus on, no matter how tired she was.

The rhythm of the machine mesmerized her, and she blinked. If she wasn't careful, she'd nod off and tumble into the apparatus. She stifled a yawn. Sleep had been elusive last night, and Nadine hadn't slept much better, getting up twice.

How had Ernst fared? After determining that Nadine was all right, he'd ducked out into the darkness. Had he been successful in getting agreements from the other farmers to act as boardinghouses? Nadine had been excited about the opportunity because it gave her the chance to contribute to the coffers. Tobias also wanted to move forward with the idea. She'd been the last holdout, not wanting Nadine to be overworked. Her sister scoffed at that comment. She had to cook and clean for the three of them. Why not for a few more? After dinner, they'd wandered through the house and decided to use their parent's room and Ilsa's. She would move into Nadine's room, so they could house two boarders. Tobias offered to sleep in the barn to free up another space, but Wisconsin winters were too cold to consider that arrangement. Two would be enough to start. What would it be like to have strangers living with them?

The door at the far end of the room opened, and Ernst stepped through, a broad smile on his face. Ilsa's heart sped up, and moisture sprang out on her palms. She licked her lips and tried not to stare as he ambled down the aisle, stopping occasionally to speak to one of the machine operators. He gestured toward Mr. Davison who wended his way toward him. The two men conferred for a moment, then Mr. Davison nodded and clapped his hands. "Ladies, please gather round. Mr. Webber has an announcement from Mr. Beck."

Ilsa flipped the switch to put her machine on standby and exchanged a look with Zlata, who shrugged. The other girls' expressions were a mixture of excitement, curiosity, and suspicion, the latter mostly from Yasmina and her compatriots. Did the woman trust no one?

Ernst held up his hands, and the murmur of conversation ceased. He beamed at them, then cleared his throat. "Thank you for your attention, ladies. I'll just be a moment. First of all, I want to pass along Mr. Beck's compliments of your hard work. He appreciates all that you've done and continue to do to make his company a success. You have exceeded our expectations and your quotas, and you should be very proud of yourselves."

Yasmina mumbled something under her breath, and Ernst pursed his lips. She blushed, then ducked her head.

He continued, "Because of our growth, there are several new positions open within the company. The descriptions will be posted in the break rooms so you can see what is available. Everyone is encouraged to apply for any job in which you're interested. Some are within other departments, and a few are supervisory positions."

"Since when does Mr. Beck want us to be managers?" Yasmina raised her hand and appeared skeptical.

"Since now." Ernst smiled at her, then swept his gaze over the group, his eyes resting on Ilsa for an extra second. "Mr. Beck is very progressive, and he believes in putting the best person into the job, male or female."

"He hasn't done so yet." A voice came from the back of the crowd. "Why should we believe you?"

"That's true. He has not, and in my recent meeting with him, he expressed his chagrin for that practice. He realized this is the perfect opportunity to remedy the situation. As far as whether or not you think he's telling the truth, you'll have to take my word for it, or wait and see for yourselves. Although, if you don't apply, you'll be missing a wonderful chance for a new and perhaps higher paying job."

Mumbling swelled as the women talked among themselves.

"Any questions?" Ernst pierced Yasmina with a look, but she remained silent. No one spoke, so he bowed slightly. "Thank you for your time. Anyone interested in being considered should submit a letter of intent to Mr. Davison at front office no later than Friday."

The women dispersed and went back to their machines.

"Ilsa, a moment."

She turned and worried her lower lip with her teeth. Why did he always call her out in front of others? Did he not realize he embarrassed her with the attention? She forced a smile glad the other women were no longer close enough to hear the conversation. "Yes?"

"One of the new openings is to replace Mr. Davison as the supervisor for this department, and I wanted to encourage you to apply."

"What? Is he leaving?"

"No, Mr. Beck would like to move him to another position. I'm not sure where. You'd be perfect."

"I'm not sure about that, but I'm happy working the machine."

"And you're very good, which is why you'd make an excellent supervisor."

She shook her head. "Don't you understand? I can't. The girls have seen us talking, and if I get the job, they'll think you're playing favorites. Again. My relationship with some of them is difficult enough without adding misconceptions into the mix."

"But I have nothing to do with the decision. Mr. Beck asked me to make the announcement, but he's the one who will interview and select the individuals. There are other girls in here who should apply for other positions. Your friend Zlata comes to mind. Invite her to submit a letter."

Ilsa studied him for a moment. He seemed to honestly want her and Zlata, and perhaps others to get ahead in the company. Why did she continue to suspect his motives? When had she gotten so cynical?

##

Ernst swallowed a sigh. Ilsa continued to throw up barriers. Not all the time, but at the least expected moment. After the first few days on the special project, they'd worked together with ease, slipping into their old camaraderie. Sometimes, she'd nod and bestow a smile on him if they passed in the corridor or parking lot. Occasionally, she allowed him to strap her bicycle to the back of his carriage so he could drive her home. Other times, like today, she reacted like a he had an infectious disease.

"Apparently, I didn't make myself clear." He gestured to Mr. Davison. "I need to straighten out some confusion."

The man nodded, put two fingers between his lips, and whistled. As one, the women's heads jerked toward him. He beckoned them toward him and shouted, "We have further information."

They left their machines and shuffled across the floor.

"Miss Krause indicated that perhaps I haven't made myself clear, and I apologize. I have nothing to do with the hiring process. Mr. Beck asked me to make the announcement because he was anxious for you to hear it and would be unable to inform you himself until tomorrow. Anyway, what I haven't seemed to convey is that he will be the one speaking with the applicants and selecting the candidates. His managers and I have nothing to do with the process other than to let you know about the jobs and to urge you to apply if you feel you are ready for a different challenge."

"Mr. Beck himself will talk to us?" Zlata's voice wobbled. "Why would he do that?"

"An excellent question, Miss Petric. He has a particular vision for his company and feels he's in the best position to choose those workers who will be able to implement it. He also wants to meet everyone, so that he can be aware of those who might not be a fit now, but would be a great choice down the road."

"I still don't think he's going to pick any of us." Olya frowned. "He's going through the motions to make it look good, like he cares for us women, but when all is said and done, he'll say we're not qualified."

"Yeah, men don't hire women as supervisors, so none of us has experience. That will give him an easy out."

"I assure you that he's looking for potential." Ernst pointed to himself. These women were more jaded than any lawyer he'd ever met. He had to convince them. "I had no management experience when he hired me. I was fresh out of college. Yes, I had good grades, but none of my summer jobs put me in charge of anyone. So, you see, he is willing to take a chance on the uninitiated."

He finger-combed his hair. "Before you discount this chance, think about all that Mr. Beck has done to improve the community. Before he ever hired a soul, he built housing for employees as well as created the support structures necessary for people to live. We have shops of all kinds, parks, schools, and a hospital. He *invested* in you before he brought you on board. He is successful and wealthy, so perhaps it's difficult to believe that he cares, but he does. He came from nothing, and he wants to give a hand to those behind him."

Mr. Davison clapped him on the back. "He did the same for me. I'd worked for the railroads. Never bossed anyone in my life, but he must have seen something and gave me a chance."

"Check the newspapers," Ernst said. "There are plenty of company towns that are run poorly with no thought to the welfare of the employees. I won't name names, but be honest with yourselves. Mr. Beck is different. His town is different."

"So are you telling us that we'll be over the men? How will that work?" someone asked from the back.

"Again, my apologies for not being clear. Women will supervise women and men will supervise men."

A couple of women snorted a laugh. "The men are not going to be happy seeing us gals get ahead."

"Then they can leave." Ernst raised his chin. "Mr. Beck has made it clear that he intends to pick women to manage this department and several others that employ only women. And the fellas can get on board or leave. I will be frank with you. Mrs. Beck is the one who suggested that he hire and promote women. As many of you know, she is an outspoken suffragist."

"A formidable force," Mr. Davison quipped.

A chuckle flowed through the group.

Ernst grinned. "Indeed. I'd like to have overheard those conversations, myself. Anyway, Mr. Beck is willing to support her...and you...in this, but it is up to you to want to succeed."

"But how? We just said we don't have experience." Ilsa crossed her arms. "We'll fail before we start."

"Anyone selected will be trained. Just like I was, and Mr. Davison. But you must be willing to learn, to put in the hours and the commitment. He wants you to do well; your success is beneficial to the company. A happy and engaged employee is the best resource an organization can have, man or woman. Promoting you ladies is the right thing to do, and hopefully someday the practice will be a normal part of business rather than an anomaly." Ernst glanced at Ilsa who appeared stunned at his declaration. With any luck, his own surprise at his words wasn't evident on his face. He hadn't realized until he blurted out the statement that he truly believed what he was saying.

Chapter Twelve

Arms crossed, Ilsa stood in the doorway of her parents' bedroom and surveyed the spacious room. Her heart clenched, and tears pricked the backs of her eyes. She'd removed all of their personal items and hung a small quilt on one wall. One of the shops in town had a sale on curtains, so she replaced her mother's lacy sheers with more masculine navy-blue cotton drapes, and they could be used to block the light if necessary. She'd purchased green ones for her room that had also been converted for the anticipated boarders. An employee from the company had dropped off the men's trunks shortly after breakfast.

In the corner stood the washstand that Tobias had sanded and painted a warm shade of cinnamon. The brown-sponged pitcher and basin blended nicely with the rest of the décor. There was nothing more she could do to prepare, so she wandered across the hall into the room she'd vacated.

Memories washed over her. Mornings of waking up to the sound of Mama's and Papa's voices. Afternoons sitting at her desk doing schoolwork. Nights curled up on the bed with a book. The space no longer resembled her girlhood bedroom. Most of her things had been moved to

Nadine's room. The rest of the items had been packed into boxes and stored in the barn loft.

She trailed her fingers along the bed as she walked to the window. Looking through the branches of the tree outside, her face heated. She'd allowed herself to be talked into sneaking out of the house to attend the school play, one her parents had forbidden her to see, and now she couldn't remember the title. Claiming a headache, she'd gone to her room, then shinnied down the trunk and cycled into town to meet her friends. Papa had been waiting at the base of the tree when she returned. Instead of hollering at her, he'd drawn her into his arms and explained that he was trying to keep her safe from the world. He asked her to trust him when he felt there was something she shouldn't do. What she wouldn't give to be sheltered in his embrace at the moment.

"Oh, Papa. Why did you have to leave us?" Her voice wobbled, and she swallowed against the lump that had formed in her throat. "I miss you."

Movement in the yard caught her attention, and she watched Tobias head toward the lower field, pulling a cart filled with fence repair equipment. His broad shoulders bunched with the effort, but he seemed unaffected. His hat was pushed back on his head, and he walked with a spring in his step. Every now and then he cast a glance at the sunny sky.

He'd worked wonders on the farm in the few months since Papa's death. There was still a tremendous amount of work to do, but he'd attacked each task with joy and excitement, and the improvements were evident everywhere she looked. She'd failed to tell him how proud she was of all he'd done.

From downstairs, she heard the cuckoo clock chirp four times. The timepiece was one of the few items her grandparents brought from Germany when they came. Satisfied there was nothing else she could do to prepare the rooms, she left and ascended the stairs to her new bedroom. Ernst would arrive at any moment.

Her pulse sped up, and she opened the closet to select a clean dress. Telling herself she wanted to ensure she looked her best for the new boarders, she shook her head. She wasn't kidding anyone, least of all herself. Peeling off the plain cotton work dress, she stood in front of the closet in her shift and rifled through the garments. Nothing appealed, so she yanked her favorite yellow dress from the hanger. The color of jonquils, the gown had a lace collar and cuffs and a large ruffle at the bottom of the skirt.

After donning the outfit, she checked her appearance in the mirror and grimaced at her reflection. Tendrils of hair had pulled from her bun and sprang out in all directions. A smudge of dirt marred her forehead. With quick motions, she cleaned her face, then removed the pins and brushed her blonde locks, braiding them into one long plait. Her heightened color gave her no need to pinch her cheeks.

"Ilsa!" Nadine called from the kitchen. "Do you have time to set the table? Our guests will be arriving soon."

"Coming!" She couldn't stall any longer, so she poked her feet into a pair of low-heeled shoes. "Ready or not," she mumbled under her breath. She went into the corridor and closed the door behind her. Pressing one hand against her middle, she grasped the railing with the other hand and headed downstairs. Entering the kitchen, she inhaled deeply. "You've outdone yourself. It smells divine."

Already flushed, her sister's face deepened. "I want to make a good impression."

"You're a wonderful cook. They're lucky to be staying here." She gave Nadine a one-armed hug. "Then you want to use Mama's good dishes?"

"Yes, and I ironed the napkins and put them on the dining room table."

"You've thought of everything."

"I must. This house is a business now. I want to be taken seriously."

"And so you shall." She pushed through the swinging door into the dining room. Nadine had used her egg money to purchase new wallpaper that she'd hung herself. A burgundy background was offset by sage-colored leaves and mauve blossoms. She also repainted all the trim, giving the room a crisp and fresh image. The rug needed to be replaced, but there were no more funds for upgrades.

She opened the sideboard, the last piece of furniture her grandfather had made. Constructed of beechwood, the piece had four intricately carved doors with copper handles, and a gleaming top. Grandfather had spent hours sanding and rubbing tung oil into the surface. Reaching inside, she withdrew the plates Mama only used for special occasions. She traced the blue onion pattern on the delicate china before laying a plate on the table in front of each chair, then added napkins and silverware to each place setting. Fortunately, the mild fall weather had been kind to the few late-blooming black-eyed Susans, and Nadine had arranged them in a pitcher and tied a ribbon around the handle.

A door slammed in the back of the house, then Tobias's heavy tread came toward her. She looked up as he entered the room, dirty and disheveled. He held up one hand. "Before you bark at me, I know I'm late, but one of the pastures had a break in the fence. It couldn't wait."

"I saw you through my window. I knew it was important for you to take care of it so late in the day." She hurried toward him and kissed his cheek, the stubble on his face tickling her lips. "It reminded me that I haven't told you how proud I am of all you've done. You work hard, and I feel safe knowing you are in the house."

He pinked to the roots of his hair. "Thanks. That means a lot. There are days I feel I'll never measure up to Papa's standards."

"I feel the same about Mama's, but we are doing a good job, and we have to make our own way. Do what works for us as a family." She pinched the bridge of her nose and waved her hand. "Now, go clean up. We don't want to frighten our new boarders. They'll see you in all your glory soon enough."

With a guffaw, he winked, then spun on his heel and marched from the room, his laughter fading as she ducked back into the kitchen. "Ready in there? How about if I watch the food while you go and freshen up?"

Panic etched lines in Nadine's face. "Do I look that awful?"

"Of course not. You'd look lovely in a flour sack, but you've been working since sunup. You'll feel better if you splash some water on your face and put on another dress."

"All right. Thanks." Her sister untied her apron, tossed it on the back of a chair, and rushed from the kitchen, her shoes slapping on the wooden floor. "Keep an eye on the cornbread. It should come out of the oven in a few minutes," she called from a distance.

Ilsa hummed as she peeked into the lone pot on top of the stove. Fluffy mashed potatoes waited to be doused with butter. The roast was done and sat in the pan, surrounded by carrots, parsnips, and turnips. On the counter, frosted apple cake emitted a sugary-sweet aroma.

Minutes later, Nadine and Tobias walked into the kitchen as a knock sounded on the front door. Ilsa's heart stuttered, and she wiped her palms on her skirt. Nadine's eyes widened, her the only indication of her nerves. Tobias rubbed his hands together and grinned. "Let the fun begin."

She swatted his arm. "Behave yourself."

"I'll be the ultimate gentleman farmer." He executed a mock bow. "After you, ladies."

They giggled, the tension seeping from the air. Nadine opened the door, and a cool breeze followed their guests inside.

Ernst pointed first to the taller of the two men, his wispy blond hair barely covering his head, then at the short, beefy man. "This is Mr. Nader. He has moved here from Michigan, and Mr. Corrigan is from Green Bay."

"It is lovely to meet you, both. I hope you'll be happy here." Nadine gestured down the hall. "Dinner is ready, and Tobias will take your coats while Ilsa and I put the food on the table. Then we can get better acquainted."

"I look forward to seeing what you've made, Nadine." Ernst rubbed his stomach. "I've been regaling the men about your cooking exploits of the past."

"Hopefully, they won't be disappointed."

"Unlikely."

Ilsa sent him a grateful smile, then followed Nadine back to the kitchen. She appreciated his efforts to set Nadine at ease. He was right. The meal would be scrumptious, and the men's rooms were comfortable and attractive.

In minutes, they'd carried the platters and bowls into the dining room and seated themselves around the table. Tobias held out his hands and looked at their guests. "We normally hold hands for the blessing, but I don't want to make you uncomfortable."

The two men shook their heads. "It is a pleasure to see that you are a family of believers."

Seated next to Ernst, Ilsa licked her lips as she took his hand in hers. His palm was warm and dry against hers. Could he feel her pulse thumping? She was being ridiculous. They were just friends. Nothing more. If only her heart could agree.

"Excellent." Tobias led them in prayer, then began to pass the various dishes around the table. "We're happy to have you staying with us."

Ernst released her hand, then smiled at her. "Just like old times."

Addled by his nearness, she nodded, then forced herself to pay attention to Mr. Nader, who was handing her the bowl of potatoes.

Across the table, Mr. Corrigan forked a slice of beef onto his plate, then passed the platter. "We were talking on the trip here that we look forward to working with you on our days off. We don't wish to be a burden."

"You're hardly that."

"Nonetheless, I grew up on a farm and know the amount of work required to keep it going. An extra pair of hands is always welcome."

"True. Thank you for your willingness to help." Tobias glanced at Mr. Nader. "Do you have farm experience?"

"No, but I can learn. My father died when I was very young, and my mother was a schoolteacher. We lived in the city all my life, but she assigned me plenty of chores." Grief clouded his face. "Her favorite saying was that idle hands were the devil's workshop."

Ilsa tilted her head. "When did you lose her?"

"Last year. She had a full life, but I miss her greatly." He cleared his throat. "I was saddened to hear about your own recent loss."

"Thank you." Gratitude and anger warred for supremacy within her. The thought of needing assistance from their boarders needled her. They should be able to succeed on their own, without outsiders. But Papa had left them in a bind, one that forced them to seek help and income from other sources. She bit her lip and forced herself to follow the chatter at the table.

Conversation continued, and time passed quickly. The boarders were polite and erudite, and topics ranged from world news to the latest inventions and advances in medicine. Ilsa couldn't remember the last time she'd spent such a delightful evening entertaining.

The clock trilled, and Ernst pulled out his pocket watch. "Goodness, is it eight o'clock already? I apologize for overstaying."

"No need to apologize, Ernst." Tobias shook his head. "This has been a much needed and welcome diversion. We should do it again sometime."

Ernst climbed to his feet. "You must let me help with the dishes."

"Shoo. All of you." Nadine gave them a saucy smile. "I don't need you men cluttering my kitchen. I'll take care of everything."

"If you insist."

"She rarely lets anyone in there, Ernst." Tobias chuckled. "Don't take it personally."

"Then I'll take my leave. Everything was delicious, Nadine. Thank you for including me."

Nadine blushed. "You're welcome any time, Ernst. Follow Tobias, and he'll show you and the men where they'll be staying."

Ernst's gaze slid to Ilsa. "See you at work on Monday."

His look seemed to caress her, and her breath caught. "You won't be at church tomorrow?" She clamped her lips together. Who was she to ask him about his attendance. "Uh, sorry."

He lowered one lid in a slow wink. "You'll miss me?"

"Well—"

"One of the shift supervisors will be out. His wife just had a baby, so I'm going to cover for him."

Tobias clapped him on the back. "Building up favors, old man? Smart move. Come on. Time's wasting. Let me show you the rooms."

"Yes, yes." With a last glance at her, he turned and followed the men from the room.

Behind her, Nadine chuckled. "You've got it bad, don't you?"

Ilsa's shoulders slumped. "Yes, and I don't know what to do about it."

"We'll figure out something." Nadine snapped her fingers. "All that talk, and I forgot to tell the men what time I'll be serving breakfast on weekends and during the week. I don't think you'll mind running up to let them know."

"Well, I might walk." She nudged her sister and sauntered toward the stairs, Nadine's laughter following her. When she reached the foyer, she picked up her pace.

Ernst's voice trickled from one of the rooms. "Please keep the information to yourselves. Mr. Beck would have my hide if this got out."

Ilsa froze. Was something wrong at the company? Why would he tell Tobias but not her or Nadine? Her stomach clenched, and dinner threatened to reappear.

Chapter Thirteen

"I look forward to working with you." Standing in the threshold of the room that Ernst assumed used to belong to Ilsa's parents, based on the large double bed, he shook Mr. Nader's hand, then Mr. Corrigan's. "I appreciate your discretion. Enjoy the rest of your weekend. We'll be at it bright and early on Monday. Meanwhile, you can discuss among yourselves which room you'd like. The other bedroom is smaller."

Mr. Nader jerked his head toward the doorway. "Mr. Corrigan is welcome to stay in here. A smaller place is perfect for me. Less to keep tidy."

With a chuckle, Mr. Corrigan said, "Smart. I wish I'd thought of that."

"We'll be quite happy here, Mr. Webber. The family is warm and friendly, and the accommodations homey and attractive. Thank you for assigning us to this house."

"You're welcome. I've known them for years. We grew up together."

"The sisters are lovely." Mr. Corrigan raised one eyebrow. "I'm surprised they have not found husbands."

Ernst clenched his teeth. Did the man have designs on Ilsa or Nadine already? He'd have to keep an eye on the situation. "Ilsa has been acting as a mother to her siblings, and Nadine is young."

"Not too young."

"Should we find other lodging for you?"

Hands held up as if in surrender, Mr. Corrigan shook his head. "Merely an observation. I'm not in the market for a wife."

"Nor I." Mr. Nader rocked on his heels. "I'm betrothed and will marry next summer. I took this job to earn enough money to purchase a home."

"Congratulations." Ernst rubbed his chest. He might have been wed by now if he hadn't cast aside Ilsa. What a fool he'd been. "Mr. Beck is very generous, and it is possible to grow within the company." He snapped his fingers. "I'll leave you to it. I've just remembered I need to cover a few things with Miss Krause...Nadine. Good night."

"Good night."

Mr. Nader walked into Ilsa's former bedroom, and Ernst glanced inside before the man closed the door. A green-and-white quilt was draped over the bed, and green curtains graced the windows. Surface gleaming, the top of the dresser was devoid of any items. A rag rug covered the floor. Was the quilt hers? Had she slept under its warmth? Or was the stitched coverlet one of many she or Nadine had created? What had it cost her to give up her personal space? Would he be willing to do the same?

He headed toward the stairs. The door to the fourth bedroom opened, and Ilsa rushed into the hallway, bumping into him. He tottered, then grabbed her arms to keep them both from falling.

Face close to his, her eyes widened, and she squealed. "I thought you'd gone." She stiffened under his touch.

Grasping her for a moment longer than he needed to, he reveled in the feel of her closeness, although he'd given up the right to hold her, years ago. She pulled away, and his face heated. He cleared his throat. "Uh, no. I was finishing up with the men. I need to see Nadine about logistics. I meant to stop by days ago to discuss everything, but time got away from me. Would you care to join us?"

"Sure." Her tone was icy. "I guess I should understand the arrangements. Give me a moment to inform the men about breakfast."

"Of course." He waited while she tapped on each door and called through the wood. The men acknowledged her, and she turned toward him. He crooked his arm, and with a nod, she drew her skirts close, then descended beside him.

What had changed since dinner when she'd been amicable and talkative? Maybe she was concerned the boarders would step into the hallway and see them. He should have thought of that. Being upstairs with her could sully her reputation. She didn't tend to care what others thought of her, but if her behavior was misconstrued, she could lose her job.

At the bottom of the stairs, she removed her hand from his arm, then walked to the kitchen and poked her head inside. "Nadine, Ernst wants to talk to us about the logistics of having the men here."

Nadine responded with a muffled assent, and a second later, appeared in the doorway, wiping her hands on a towel. "Good timing. I just finished putting the kitchen to rights. Let's go to the parlor. Did you want any coffee, Ernst?"

"No, you've worked enough for one day. Besides, I've stayed too long as it is. I'll be as quick as I can."

"Not a problem. I imagine I'll work more than a few late nights in this new venture." She smiled. "At least until I get the hang of it."

They entered the cozy room, and Ernst gaped. Several pieces of furniture had been removed, and the remaining pieces arranged into conversation clusters. The heavy drapes had been replaced with lightweight tan curtains. Family portraits had been replaced with a fabric wall hanging and a dried floral wreath.

"We wanted the boarders to feel like this was their home, too." Nadine motioned for him to sit on the sofa while she lowered herself into one of the matching chairs. "Being surrounded by our family pictures wouldn't have allowed that."

Ilsa sat in the chair next to her sister and folded her hands. Her eyes were downcast, her mouth set in a slash. What *was* she so upset about?

"Very astute of you." He crossed one leg over the other, then withdrew a folded piece of paper from his breast pocket and handed it to Nadine. "This letter outlines everything I'm about to tell you. There are two copies. One for you to sign and return, the other to keep for your records. I should have taken care of this last week."

"Were you as lax with the other families?" Ilsa twisted her lips. "Or is it just us that you take for granted?"

"Ilsa!" Nadine swatted her sister's shoulder. "We have a long and abiding friendship with Ernst and his family. It's only natural that he might be less stringent with us."

He laced his fingers together. "Yes, but she's right. This is a business relationship, and I should treat it as such. In fact, friendships can create difficulties in business dealings, so I was remiss." He slid his gaze from Nadine to Ilsa. "I hope you'll forgive the lapse in judgment."

"Nonsense. There's nothing to forgive." Nadine waved the papers. "Please proceed."

"Very well." Shifting away from Ilsa's piercing glare, Ernst focused on her sister, who'd matured and grown into a beautiful young woman since he'd left for college. Behind the sadness lurking in her eyes, a steel resolve glittered. She grieved her father's death, but at the same time seemed determined to stand on her own two feet. Why couldn't she be the one who set his heart racing? The one he was eager to see each day? Instead, he was drawn to Ilsa, stubborn and stiff-necked Ilsa who was once again upset with him for some unknown infraction. If she was so easily offended, she was not the woman for him. Besides, he'd committed himself to his career, and at this juncture, a wife had no place in his life. Especially one so temperamental. His pulse stuttered as a thought sprang into his mind. Had she been upstairs while he was talking with the men? Had she heard their conversation? If so, she could easily derail his plans.

Chapter Fourteen

Seated next to Nadine, Ilsa watched the interplay between her and Ernst. When had her sister grown up? Elegant and self-assured, she looked every inch the savvy businesswoman. She'd entertained the boarders during dinner, introducing interesting topics to prompt discussion when conversation lagged. Hair swept into a simple chignon, her cheeks were rosy and her eyes bright. Her pink dress, although simple, accented her lithe figure and complemented her coloring.

Worrying her lower lip between her teeth, Ilsa sighed. She'd overreacted and thrown snide questions at Ernst. Of course, he was more relaxed in his dealings with them. She should have appreciated his consideration instead of criticizing him. He must think her a shrew.

She pressed a hand against her middle. Why couldn't she get her emotions under control? Her sister had matured, but what about herself? Rather than make assumptions from the few words she'd heard that he had nefarious plans, she should mind her own business. He is a manager in the company as are their boarders. He had every right to tell them things and caution the men to keep the information confidential.

Another sigh escaped, and she clamped her lips together. She straightened her spine and blinked. *Focus!*

"The company will keep track of the number of employees you will board as well as the number of days per month each individual stays with you. You'll be paid on the fifth of each month for the preceding month. You're welcome to pick up the check, or you can have it mailed to you, whichever is more convenient." Ernst reached into his breast pocket and withdrew a check that he gave to Nadine. "Mr. Beck recognizes that there are expenses you may have incurred to prepare the house for his men, so here's a check that will hopefully cover most of your costs."

Ilsa gaped at him. Mr. Beck's generosity continued to astound her.

Ernst glanced at her, then back at Nadine. "He has done this for all the families who will be boarding employees."

She flushed. He obviously meant the comment for her.

"Before you leave, I'd like to write a thank-you note to him." Nadine tucked the check into the folded letter. "This will allow me to make further improvements."

"I don't see anything else that needs to be done. Your home is lovely, but use the money as you see fit. There are no stipulations on it." He tugged on his jacket sleeves. "As discussed at dinner, the men are expected to help around the house and farm. They're to keep their rooms tidy and help with chores. It sounds like Mr. Corrigan may be of more help initially because of his background in farming. But Mr. Nader seems eager enough to learn, although I'm sure there are enough tasks that require little skill."

Ilsa frowned. "I still don't see why we have to let them work for us. We're capable of getting things done on our own." Irritation flitted across his face, and she swallowed. She'd been critical and complaining again, after she'd just reprimanded herself for those very behaviors. *Lord, forgive me and help me curb my tongue which has become bitter and sharp of late.* "I'm sorry, um, we're being paid for the men's presence. It doesn't seem fair to make them work for us, too."

His features smoothed. "True, but Mr. Beck is paying on their behalf. Perhaps he wants them to work as a way to appreciate what they've been given. He doesn't share the reasons for his decisions. He expects all his boarders to assist, not just yours."

"Understood."

Nadine waved the papers. "If you have a pen, Ernst, I can sign this. I've had a chance to read it while you two sparred." Her tone was dry. "Let me handle this, sister. We each have our responsibilities, and mine are the house and its boarders. You took Mother's place and raised me to think for myself. Now is the time to let me do that. If I need your advice, or Tobias's, I'll ask for it."

"Of course. I didn't mean to suggest that you aren't capable." Ilsa sagged against the chair and avoided Ernst's eyes. "I—"

"You are trying to protect me as you are wont to do." She cradled Ilsa's hand. "I love that you've always been the ferocious mother tiger, protecting all of us, but this cub is grown up now."

"You are, indeed." Ilsa squeezed her sister's hand. "How did I miss that?"

"You were busy with your own life."

Ernst rose and gave Nadine a pen. "I believe I've worn out my welcome this evening. If you'll sign, I can be on my way."

Face warm, Ilsa sent him an apologetic smile as Nadine scrawled her signature on the page. "Ernst—"

He held up one hand and shook his head. "We've known each other too long to worry about a few sharp words. Families bicker." He winked and tucked the pen and letter back into his jacket pocket. "This isn't the first time we've had a disagreement, nor will it be our last. Good night, ladies." He ambled from the room, and a moment later, the front door opened, then closed.

Nadine got up and went to the small desk nestled in the corner of the room, then slipped the letter inside. She yawned and rotated her neck. "I'm bushed, and tomorrow morning will come early, so I'm going to bed."

"I'll join you." She pushed herself to her feet and trudged toward the door. "Listen, about what I said... I'm sorry." She huffed out a sigh. "What is wrong with me? I alternate between crying and snapping at those I care about."

A sheen of moisture sprang to Nadine's eyes, and she drew Ilsa into a hug. "It hasn't been long since Papa...died." Her voice broke. "You're grieving. We all are. Give yourself some grace."

"Hopefully, Ernst will as well."

"You're safe. I see how he looks at you."

"We're just friends, Nadine."

"You two may not have figured it out yet, but you're much more than friends." She nudged Ilsa's shoulder. "Our first night as roommates. You better not snore."

"Hey—"

Giggling, her sister raced from the room, her laughter fading as she ran up the stairs.

Ilsa sprang after Nadine, heart lighter than it had been in days. She'd set her sister straight about Ernst tomorrow. Unless, she was right.

Chapter Fifteen

Perspiration trickled between Ilsa's shoulder blades as she fumbled with the door to the hopper. Why wouldn't it open? She leaned forward and squinted at the latch. Nothing seemed amiss. Her frustration was mounting, but she stifled the desire to bang her fist on the metal door. She'd bruise her hand, and the action wouldn't solve the problem. She huffed a breath and searched the room for someone who might help her. All the girls were bent over their machines.

Except one.

Yasmina smirked at her from down the aisle. Had she sabotaged the latch? When would she have done such a deed? They'd all been hard at work since arriving three hours ago. No. The night-shift operator must have failed to fasten the door properly. Yasmina probably found Ilsa's annoyance amusing.

She returned the girl's look with a smile of her own. If anyone could fix the problem, it was her nemesis. No matter her attitude, she had excellent mechanical skills, and she didn't seem to get flustered. After a final glare at her machine, Ilsa headed toward Yasmina, whose triumphant gleam faltered at her approach.

"What do you want?"

"The hopper door is jammed, and I can't get it open."

"What's that to me?" Yasmina looked down her nose. "I've got my own machine to run."

"You're better than me at this sort of thing. I'd hoped you might give me a hand." Ilsa shrugged. "I could ask Mr. Davison, or we could get one of the men from maintenance, but I'd rather show that we girls can handle difficulties."

Indecision clouded Yasmina's eyes. She seemed to study Ilsa for an ulterior motive. "I don't understand why you picked me. You hate me."

"What?" Ilsa gaped at her. "I don't hate you. You're the one who dislikes me. Anyway, as I said, you're good at repairs."

"Fine." The girl turned off her machine and flounced down the aisle to Ilsa's station. She bent and peered at the closure, then ran her fingers along the hinges and edge of the door. She pointed to one side. "See here? It's out of alignment. I'm surprised it would latch. I'll be right back." She hurried to the far end of the room where a supply of tools was stored. Moments later, she returned with a screwdriver. "Not the most elegant of solutions." With a few deft motions, she unjammed the door and clicked open the hasp.

"You're amazing. Thank you." She patted Yasmina on the shoulder, and the woman flinched under her fingers. Ilsa removed her hand, and mumbled, "Sorry."

"Glad to help." Yasmina's face held a touch of wariness. "Thanks for asking me."

"Any time."

"This isn't break time." Mr. Davison stood in the aisle, arms crossed.

"No, sir." Ilsa motioned toward the hopper. "I couldn't get the door open, and Yasmina was kind enough to help me. We didn't want to bother you or any of the men with such a trivial problem."

His eyebrows shot to his hairline. "You girls fixed it?"

"Not me. Yasmina. She's a whiz with stuff like this."

"Hmm. Well done, Miss Carle. I'll note your work in my logs. Get back to your station."

"Yes, sir." She shot Ilsa a satisfied smile. Not exactly warm and friendly, but not adversarial either. Perhaps a bridge had been built.

Ilsa slid the stack of foil wrappers into the receptacle, then closed and fastened the door. She nodded to Mr. Davison, then turned on the machine preventing further discussion. He pivoted on his heel and strode toward his office. She watched him from the corner of her eye. The man was a disconcerting combination of support and condescension. His tone said he was astounded that Yasmina could determine the cause of the door jam, yet on most days he treated them with respect. Who knew working with men would be so challenging?

She shook her head to clear her thoughts, and her lips twisted in a wry grin. Maybe there was good reason to keep men and women separated after all. A trio of men entered the room from the far end, and her pulse quickened. An unfamiliar man towered over the group, but she riveted her gaze on Ernst. Even from a distance, she could see that he looked her way, excitement on his face. Her mouth curved of its own accord. What news did they bring? Two weeks had passed since she'd met with Mr. Beck to discuss her application for one of the supervisory jobs. Initially terrified to meet the important man, she'd relaxed after he shared his humble beginnings. Not having worked on a farm himself, he'd seemed fascinated by the many aspects of farm life and questioned her extensively. Either Ernst had told him of her financial straits or he assumed she'd eagerly joined his company, because surprisingly, he hadn't pursued the topic.

The meeting had lasted nearly an hour and felt more like a conversation between associates than an interview. He never once spoke down to her and twice commented he was impressed with how she'd handled difficult situations. At the end, he assured her that he was pleased she was part of his organization, but made no indication that she would be selected. Even if she didn't get one of the jobs, the discussion had served to wipe away the final vestiges of bitterness at having to work at the factory. As she left the man's office, she realized he'd had nothing to do with Papa's choices, and she was being afforded an opportunity not available to many women. She needed to see her employment as the blessing it was.

Ernst beckoned to the workers, and the machines stilled as the girls hurried to gather around him. Heart pounding, Ilsa loitered on the outskirts of the crowd. Zlata bumped her shoulder and sent her an encouraging smile. Another blessing was her new friend, whom she wouldn't have met if it weren't for her job. She'd spend the bicycle ride home counting those joys and more. *Thank You, Father.*

"The good news is that we had lots of folks step forward for consideration of our open positions." Ernst rocked on his heels. "Mr. Beck spoke with each and every candidate, so the process took longer than anticipated. We thank you for your patience. It hasn't been that long since I had my own interview and experienced that excruciating wait while I wondered if I'd be selected."

A chuckle swept through the women, and Ilsa wiped her damp hands on her sleeves. The moment she'd been dreading. Would the girls make fun of her for not being picked? For having the audacity to apply?

"I'm pleased to announce that three of you have been chosen to head the wrapping department, one for each shift. Nadia Latkowski is the new manager for third shift, Fran Varley for second, and Ilsa Krause for first shift. Mr. Davison will be moving to the cocoa bean processing department."

She gasped and clapped a hand over her mouth. First shift? The most desirable of the positions, and she'd been selected. Mr. Beck thought enough of her to give her a chance.

Zlata squealed and pulled her into a tight hug. "I knew you were perfect for this job, and I'm glad they realize it, too."

"Oh, Zlata. I never thought it was possible, but am I really able to do this?"

"Absolutely. I have no doubt."

Scattered applause filled the room as Ernst asked the three new supervisors to join him, then addressed the rest of the employees. "Mr. Beck wanted to pass along his gratitude to all of you for applying. It can be scary to put yourself out there, but you were brave enough to do so. There were many more applicants than openings, but having been interviewed by him, you will be in consideration for other jobs as they become available. And available they will be, because the company continues to grow, thanks to your efforts."

Mr. Davison waved. "You have made me proud to be your manager. You work hard and do a good job. Thank you."

"Thank you, Mr. Davison."

"Good luck!"

"Thanks!"

He dipped his head in acknowledgment, then pointed to the clock. "It is early for your break, but you may go now. Your new managers will remain here to meet with Mr. Webber."

As one, the women giggled and rushed past him. He turned and extended his hand to Ilsa, then Fran, and Nadia. "Congratulations. I am most proud of you." He jerked his head at Ernst. "What he failed to announce is that your new responsibilities begin immediately."

Ilsa gaped at him.

"I can see you're all dismayed." Ernst elbowed Mr. Davison. "What *he* failed to mention is that we will be training all of you. He will go over the particulars with regard to the wrapping department, and I will be instructing you about company policies and procedures. You will be fully prepared for your new jobs."

Fran pressed a hand against her heart. "For how long?"

"For as long as it takes." He smiled. "We want you to succeed as much as you do. You will train together during the day for the remainder of this week and into the next. Once you're comfortable, we'll transfer you to your new shifts. Will that be enough time to make any necessary arrangements?"

Fran and Nadia exchanged a glance, then nodded. Ilsa stuffed her hands into the pockets of her skirt. He'd thought of everything and seemed as excited as the women about their new assignments. She nibbled the inside of her lip. Nearly two weeks together working side by side. Was she relieved or disappointed to share their time?

Chapter Sixteen

Three weeks later, Ilsa hurried down the corridor toward the wrapping room. She'd been gone almost thirty minutes. The girls knew their jobs and performed well, but company policy required her to remain on the floor constantly, with the exception of breaks and the weekly management meeting. But another policy mandated that she look presentable at all times, and she'd torn her jacket on one of the machines. Unaware she'd caught the fabric on the hopper, she turned and the entire seam opened. Rather than risk being caught in such a state, she'd returned to the uniform room for a new coat. Then two of the new female managers stopped her for questions. As if she were the expert. Hardly.

She huffed a breath. The balancing act of doing her job within the confines of the company's many rules and regulations was a challenge she hadn't anticipated. Foolishly, she'd assumed she'd have more flexibility as a supervisor.

Nearly a month had passed since her promotion, but this was her first week of being on her own. She'd spent the two weeks after the announcement with Ernst, Mr. Davison, and staff from the administrative offices training her, and the other recently appointed managers. In addition to learning the story of Mr. Beck's rise to fame in the industry because of his development of milk chocolate, she and the others had been taught the process of chocolate-making itself and how every machine in the building worked. They also spent hours learning skills ranging from leading employees to making decisions. The tedious part of the job was the amount of required paperwork. Countless logs and reports to track progress or the lack thereof for each department were due daily and weekly.

As much as she disliked the administrative work, she was adept at it. Her penmanship had always been good as well as her attention to detail. Today was the first time she'd completed her weekly report by herself. She'd come in early to take care of it so she wouldn't be tardy if a problem arose, which was a certainty on any given day. Twice, she'd already had to work on the line after Olya called in sick.

Entering the room, her gaze ricocheted from one workstation to the next. No one looked in her direction, and nothing seemed out of place. The machines' rhythmic clatter bounced off the walls and floor with no hiccups, but she'd wander past and check to be sure.

Sauntering down the aisle, she surveyed each machine and worker. Periodically, one of the girls would look up, some smiling, others expressionless. Fortunately, no one seemed outright hostile, but she knew a few of her former coworkers were not happy that she was now their boss. During training, Ernst had talked about the possibility that some people might resent the new managers' advancement. He advised them to remain professional and to avoid getting into discussions about why they were chosen and their colleagues were not. They were to refer those conversations to him or to Mr. Beck. Easier said than done, but it was nice that she had their support.

Zlata grinned and dipped her head in acknowledgment. "How is my new boss doing? You look tired."

"Tired is a way of life." Ilsa shrugged. "Truth be told, I'm somewhat anxious. I don't want to make mistakes."

"Surely, they don't expect you to be perfect so soon."

"No, it's my own expectation."

"Which is probably why you were selected. Mr. Beck knew you would do your best."

"Thank you." Ilsa glanced over her shoulder. "I've been helping with the harvest at night. The farmers have banded together and are sharing the workload, but the crops are plentiful, and there is more produce to bring in this year."

"Praise the Lord."

"Amen." Ilsa peered at her friend. "How are you doing?"

"Fine, as always." Zlata shot her eyes to the next workstation across the aisle. "The new girl is excellent. She will soon outpace me."

"I find that hard to believe. You're the best."

Zlata pinked and shook her head. "Not anymore, but I do surpass my quota, so I am pleased."

"You trained her well, if she is better than her teacher." Ilsa squeezed Zlata's arm. "I miss taking our breaks together. Can you come to the farm for dinner tomorrow night?"

Confusion clouded Zlata's eyes. "Am I allowed to be your friend outside of work? People might think you are treating me as a favorite. Besides, aren't you going to the Oktoberfest event?"

"I hadn't thought about the perception of others." Ilsa frowned. "How frustrating that the company's rules are affecting my personal life." She brightened. "You should try to become a supervisor, then we could play together."

"I am not management material, but thank you for saying that."

"Nonsense. You are smart and good at your job. People like you. What more is necessary?"

"I don't know...anyway, enough about me. Are you going to the party?"

Cocking her head, Ilsa narrowed her eyes. "I hadn't planned on it. Are you?"

"No, I promised my friend from packaging I would stay with her elderly mother, so she could cope." She smirked. "She likes one of the men from maintenance, and she is hoping to catch his attention."

Ilsa laughed. "Good for her. Well, I must get back to my work."

Zlata nodded. "I pray for you every day, Ilsa."

"That means a lot. Thank you." Ilsa's heart lightened as she turned and headed toward her desk. As she approached, she gasped. Her weekly report was shredded. Torn into tiny pieces, the papers were piled in the middle of the scarred surface. Who would do such a thing? Zlata hadn't mentioned the incident. How could she not have seen what happened? Was she only pretending to care about her? No, that wasn't possible.

Ilsa's shoulders stiffened, and she straightened her spine. She couldn't let whoever did this see her reaction, so she grabbed the waste basket and brushed the jumble of pages into the bin. Pulling out her chair with great care, she lowered herself onto the seat and retrieved her ledger from the center drawer. She'd have to create the report all over again. Checking the watch on her jacket, she cringed. Less than an hour to finish.

She opened the book, then raised her head and scrutinized the workers. Most were bent over their machines, oblivious to her examination. Her gaze slid from machine to machine. Who was the culprit? After asking for Yasmina's help with her machine, they seemed to have arrived at a truce. The girl no longer made snide comments, but was that because of self-preservation rather than positive feelings? As her manager, Ilsa could now discipline her for unacceptable behavior.

At the far end of the room, two employees who'd been with the company since its inception stared at her. Were they responsible? Nothing in their past lent credence to that possibility. The pair kept to themselves and did their jobs, always on time and meeting their quotas. They seemed to neither like nor dislike her. But had they seen the deed done?

Conjecture was useless. More importantly, time spent speculating meant fewer minutes to get her reports ready by the deadline. She forced her attention away from the floor and turned her gaze to the ledger. Moments later, she was engrossed in compiling the information.

Her pencil scratched across the page as she transferred the numbers to the columns. Eyes burning, she blinked in an effort to clear her vision. Nearly done. Footsteps sounded, and she looked up. Ernst. Her gaze flew to the clock behind him. Drat! Why did he have to be so prompt? She still had a half page to complete.

"Miss Krause." He lifted one eyebrow. "I'm here to collect your reports, but it appears you are not finished. Disappointing."

"My apologies. I'll be a few more minutes. May I bring this to your office?"

He frowned. "I'm surprised at your tardiness. We discussed the critical nature of these reports during your training. Mr. Beck makes decisions based on the information, and he must not be kept waiting."

"I understand."

"Do you really? Frankly, being late isn't in your nature. Are you finding the position too much? I thought you'd be able to keep up with the workload. Perhaps Mr. Beck misjudged you."

"He did not." Ilsa spoke through gritted teeth. How dare he talk down to her. She'd bite off her tongue before tattling on her staff, but she didn't appreciate being dressed down for something that wasn't her fault. "Would you like me to apologize to him personally for my poor performance?"

"No." He sighed. "But I need to know if you think you'll be unable to keep up."

She rose so she could look him in the eye. "I am more than capable to do this job. I had some unforeseen difficulties, but I will ensure I am prepared in the future. Meanwhile, if you would stop reprimanding me, I could finish my report. Would you like to come back for it or wait while I finish? I'll be five minutes at most."

He stepped back and pursed his lips. "I'll return after I've collected the other reports."

"Very well."

"Oh, and one more thing." He snapped his fingers. "You'll need to come thirty minutes early to the Oktoberfest. Mr. Beck likes to spend extra time with the management team."

"I hadn't planned to attend."

"Out of the question. You're required to come."

"But—"

"Unless you or one of your family members is deathly ill, we in management are expected to appear at the various social events held by the company." He rubbed the back of his neck. "I'll be picking up your boarders at five o'clock. You're welcome to join us."

"Fine." She gestured to the papers on her desk. "Now, if you'll excuse me."

He flushed, then turned on his heel and strode from the room.

Ilsa clenched her pencil, and it snapped. She tossed it into the bin and grabbed another. Why did their interactions always seem to turn adversarial? One minute she couldn't wait to see him, the next she was barking at him like a rabid dog. She'd felt he'd been condescending, but had she overreacted out of guilt for being unprepared, even if the situation had been out of her control?

Chapter Seventeen

Staring at her reflection, Ilsa frowned, then tossed the garment she'd been holding in front of her on top of the collection of dresses, skirts, and blouses she'd already thrown on the bed. She felt like Goldilocks. A riot of color, fabrics, and styles, yet none of the items were right. Some were tired looking, others not the right color. Two of the dresses had frayed hems. She'd never cared about fashion until now. How fancy was she expected to appear? Would her choice of attire impact how she was viewed as a manager?

She sank onto the mattress with a sigh and glared at the few remaining garments hanging in the armoire. Downstairs, the cuckoo clock sang. Four o'clock. She couldn't be late, and Tobias indicated she had to be ready no later than five o'clock to make it on time. She'd turned down Ernst's offer to join him and the boarders. Riding with the three of them hadn't felt right, not that she paid attention to what others thought, but Mr. Beck might, and one woman keeping company with three single men wasn't acceptable. Why had Ernst asked? Was his request a test to see how she'd respond?

With a trembling hand, she brushed a stray lock of hair out of her face, but the tress sprang back. She rolled her eyes. She was often complimented for her thick, wavy hair, but wrestling it into place in proper Gibson Girl style never ceased to be a challenge. Why couldn't Mr. Gibson devise a look that involved short hair with no pins? Few women measured up to the man's wife or her sisters, his models for the look.

The clock chirped the quarter hour. Time was wasting, and she still hadn't figured out what to wear. She pressed her palms against her stomach that rolled and fluttered. Could she feign some terrible ailment? No, she might be anxious about tonight, but she wouldn't resort to lying to get out of attending. Besides, how bad could it be? She was a low-level supervisor. Surely, they didn't expect her to be wearing the latest gowns from New York or Paris. Or even Madison. She chuckled. Not that Wisconsin's capital was a hotbed of fashion.

"You're overthinking this, Ilsa." She shook her finger at herself in the mirror. "Get up and get dressed."

"Ilsa?" Nadine's voice was muffled on the other side of the door. "Are you ready?"

"No, but come in anyway."

Her sister entered, then shut the door with a bang. "Uh-oh, having trouble deciding what to wear?"

"Ridiculous, isn't it?" Ilsa twisted her lips. "Oktoberfest is the first event I'm attending as a manager, and I want to make a good impression. Is that silly or what? I've already got the job. Who cares what I look like?"

"You're not being silly. Of course your appearance is important." She bent and rifled through the clothes on the bed. "You have several lovely choices, but I've got just the thing." She strode across the room, yanked open her wardrobe, then pulled out a teal-colored skirt and matching blouse. Puffed at the top, the sleeves featured lace at the cuffs. More lace covered the high-necked bodice and adorned the hem of the skirt. "This will bring out the tints of green in your eyes."

"I can't borrow that." Ilsa shook her head. "You've only worn it twice."

"And I'll wear it again. It's a better color for you anyway." She pushed the garment into Ilsa's arms. "Put this on, then I'll do your hair."

"All right. If you insist."

Nadine grinned. "Of course I do." She went to the bureau and retrieved the corset. "I hope you don't plan to eat much tonight. Mr. Gibson obviously never had to wear any of his designs."

Giggling, Ilsa nodded. "I was thinking the same thing before you came in. What a price to pay for beauty, eh?"

"Indeed, but you look like Mama and are beautiful no matter what you wear."

"I miss her, especially on days like today. Do you think she's watching?"

"Tobias is the theologian. We'd have to ask him, but I'd like to think she is." Nadine gave her a tremulous smile. "Now, enough reminiscing. The longer you take, the less time I have for your hair."

"Yes, ma'am." Ilsa sent her a mock salute, then slipped out of her shift and into the corset. "You'll have to do me up, but give me enough room to breathe."

Her sister laughed, and Ilsa's heart lightened. No matter what happened tonight, she had this moment of closeness with Nadine who always knew the right thing to say and do. Moments later, she was dressed and seated at the vanity. With deft motions, her sister brushed her hair and swept it into an impeccable pompadour with waves and curls that accented the contours of her face. She turned her head to the right, then left. "I barely recognize myself."

"You'll have to tell me Ernst's reaction after you get home." Nadine clapped her hands. "I can't wait to hear."

"There'll be nothing to tell. We're colleagues. Nothing more."

"I doubt that, but if not, this is the perfect opportunity to catch his eye."

"And why would I want to do that?"

Nadine bent and met her gaze in the mirror. " Because you still care for him, whether or not you want to admit that fact. Because he is handsome, successful, and a man of faith. Because you two are perfect for each other. Because—"

"Stop." Ilsa held up her hand. "I need to focus on my job, not my love life, and certainly not a romance that includes a coworker. Mr. Beck would frown on that."

"How do you know? Does the company have rules about courting?"

"I don't know, but they have rules about everything else."

"Well, you should check. You can't stay unmarried forever, and Ernst won't be single for long."

"He's not interested in getting married. He said as much during one of the shifts when we worked on the special project."

Eyebrows wiggling, Nadine tapped her chin with one finger. "So, you talked about marriage. That bodes well. What else did you discuss? Children? Where you'd like to live?"

"Hardly." Ilsa rose and smoothed her skirts, then hugged her sister. "Thanks for helping me get ready. I feel like a princess."

"I'm glad to help, Cinderella. Just be home by midnight, and if you leave one of your shoes behind, the prince will be forced to come see if it fits."

"You're letting your imagination run away with you. The *prince* isn't interested in me, not that way, not anymore." Her chest ached, and a lump formed in her throat. Too many years had passed for them to return to the unbridled joy of being young adults, when problems like finances and career aspirations seemed far away.

"Then it is up to you to ensure he gets interested."

Ilsa swallowed a sigh. Why did life have to be so complicated?

##

Ernst pulled out his pocket watch for the umpteenth time and popped it open. Three minutes later since the last time he checked. He shoved the timepiece away and swallowed a sigh. He forced a smile, then nodded as if he'd heard everything Mr. Nader had said. If he didn't pay attention, he might get into trouble by agreeing to something he couldn't abide.

Nervous laughter came from the corner where three new female supervisors huddled. The women were barely recognizable in their gowns and upswept hair. Pretty enough, they couldn't hold a candle to Ilsa. What would she wear? His mind reviewed the outfits he'd seen her wear during high school which would be nothing like the clothes she'd wear as an adult. Shades of green were her best color, bringing out the peridot color of her eyes and highlighting her ash-blonde hair and fair complexion.

Mr. Beck circulated among the staff, his booming voice carrying across the room. He welcomed each individual and complimented the recently promoted managers. Rather than discuss work, he questioned them about their families and off-hour activities. A perpetual salesman, he'd have their loyalty if he didn't already. He knew what to say to put them at ease.

Mr. Nader said something, and Randall Rawlings chuckled. Ernst slid his gaze to the men. He really needed to pay attention. The door behind him opened, and he pivoted. Mr. Johnstone and Mr. Norris, the managers from packaging. His shoulders slumped. What was wrong with him? He was as nervous as a cat in a roomful of rocking chairs. He tugged on his sleeves, then ran his finger around his collar. The room was stifling.

"You all right, Webber?" Mr. Norris peered at him. "You look like a freshman cadet before his first review."

"I'm fine." Ernst stiffened. "I heard your department soared past your quotas. You must be proud, and Mr. Beck must be thrilled."

Mr. Norris preened. "Yep. The two new men are the hardest workers I've ever known. Their performance has prompted the others to increase their output."

"Don't work them too hard."

"Not to worry. They're big and brawny. I've not seen them tired yet."

"Wrapping seems to be doing well under Miss Krause. Labeling, too." Mr. Johnstone twisted his lips. "I must admit, I thought Beck a fool for promoting women into management, but he might be onto something. Frankly, I'm glad I don't have to worry the gals. Too emotional for my taste. You can reprimand the men, and they won't cry."

"A soft voice goes a long way." Ernst shrugged. "You wouldn't have them crying if you treated them differently."

"I shouldn't have to. They're in the workforce now. A man's world. If they can't handle it, they should leave." Rawlings cocked his head. "You learn that patter at your fancy college, Webber?"

"No, at my father's knee. He commanded respect without shouting."

"Oh, well, you do what works for you and keep your nose out of my business."

"Gentlemen, no need to argue." Mr. Corrigan held up his hands. "Oktoberfest is a time of celebration. Let's discuss topics other than work, shall we?"

Ernst dipped his head. "Happy to."

Rawlings grunted.

Musicians on the dais at the far end of the room tuned their instruments, and Ernst narrowed his eyes. He'd not seen these men before. Had Mr. Beck brought them in from out of town? Would they play tunes other than the traditional German polkas and oompa songs? Only one way to be sure.

"Excuse me." He sauntered toward the quintet, nodding to other guests as he passed. Where was Ilsa? Had she changed her mind about attending? Surely, she wouldn't jeopardize her position by being late, or worse, being absent. He approached the instrumentalists. "Good evening and welcome."

The men nodded and murmured greetings. The trumpet player stepped off the platform. "May we help you, sir?"

"I wondered what sort of repertoire you provide."

"Mr. Beck has asked for a variety of music. We will play the usual Bavarian tunes, but he's also asked for some waltzes. Apparently, those are his wife's favorite."

"Excellent." Ernst rubbed his palms together. Thank goodness for Mrs. Beck. Waltzes were his favorite as well, and his arms well-remembered the feel of Ilsa gliding across the floor in his embrace. As if conjured by his memories, she appeared in the doorway, and he gaped at her, his mouth dry.

Her teal-colored dress draped over her lithe figure, and her thick blonde hair was piled on her head in a swirl of waves. A tendril dangled on either side of her face, and his fingers itched to rub the gleaming strands to see if they were still as soft as he remembered.

He'd been a fool to think he'd outgrown her or that his career was more important. His arrogance knew no bounds. He understood that now. An excellent judge of character, she'd seen his true caliber. No wonder she'd held him at arm's length. As beautiful as she was on the outside, her spirit was even more so. Gracious, considerate, and compassionate, she never held herself above another. A servant, yet a leader.

Before he could change his mind, he strode across the floor, then stopped in front of her and bowed. "Ilsa, you look lovely. I'm glad you came."

She smiled, her face shining in the flickering lamps. "You dress up well also." Her gaze flicked past him to the other guests, then back to his face. "I hardly recognize everyone. I understand why Mr. Beck does this. We see each other differently, don't we?"

"Most definitely." He licked his lips. "Uh, before you get swept away by the others...may I have a dance or two? In addition to the traditional Oktoberfest tunes, the musicians will be playing some waltzes after dinner. Mrs. Beck's favorite."

"Are we expected to dance?" She cocked her head. "As managers?"

"No. Attendance is all that is mandatory."

Her smiled widened. "Then, yes, one dance."

His breath whooshed out. She'd agreed to a dance. Could he talk her into a second? "Thank—"

"Ilsa!" Three of the new female managers jostled him as they enveloped her. They giggled and talked, their words tumbling over each other.

"It's about time you got here."

"Where did you get that dress. It's fantastic."

"Look at your hair."

She sent him an apologetic glance as they swept her away.

He grinned and waved, then strolled toward Mr. Beck who was surrounded by several of the senior managers, his wife on his arm. By ensuring the founder saw him in attendance, he could enjoy the rest of the evening. He rolled his shoulders, then straightened his spine. As he approached, Mr. Beck caught his eye and dipped his head. Excellent. Task completed. Ernst leaned close to the man. "I believe everyone is here, sir, if you'd like to address them."

"Thank you, Mr. Webber. Perhaps after a while. Tonight is about enjoyment, not business."

"Yes, sir."

Mrs. Beck held out her hand. "Nice to see you again, Mr. Webber."

"And you, Mrs. Beck." He blinked, then shook her hand. Unusual behavior for a woman, but he'd heard about her suffragist notions. He cleared his throat. "I understand I have you to thank for ensuring the orchestra plays some waltzes."

"Your favorite, too? A young man with taste."

His face warmed. Did she think he was trying to ingratiate himself? "My mother taught me. It is her favorite as well."

"I think I'd like your mother."

"I know you would. I don't wish to commandeer your time, so please excuse me."

"Of course. Enjoy your evening."

He wandered along the edge of the room, stopping periodically to chat with his coworkers. Time passed, and Mr. Beck gave a short speech, thanking the managers for their hard work and productivity, then congratulated the new managers on their progress. The rest of the employees trickled into the room, some of the men wearing the traditional lederhosen, and two women attired in dirndls. What would Ilsa look like in one of the folk dresses?

A buffet was laid out, and he availed himself of some of the food while trying not to count the minutes until the dancing would begin.

"We're sorry, Miss Krause."

Ernst's head whipped around toward the voice. A few yards away, Ilsa stood with two of her staff who looked contrite. What had happened? He slipped behind a large plant.

"I don't understand why you tore up my reports. Were you trying to get me in trouble or just make my job harder?"

One of the women ducked her head and mumbled, and he strained to hear her. "It was a dare. We didn't think about the fact you'd get reprimanded."

"A dare? I've treated you fairly from the very beginning and done nothing to deserve that sort of treatment."

"You're right." The other woman spoke. "We're sorry. Why didn't you tell him what we'd done to the papers?"

"Because that would have been an excuse. It's partially my fault for not securing the report. The information is confidential and should have been locked in my desk."

"We'll go to Mr. Webber and confess. He should know you're not to blame."

"No, but thank you for the offer. I appreciate you gals coming forward. We'll put this behind us."

"You're not going to have us fired?" The woman's voice was incredulous. "That's what we deserve."

"Perhaps, and I will make a note of the incident in my files, but this is your first, and hopefully only, offense. You're good workers, and you need your jobs, if I'm not mistaken. However, you will have to regain my trust. Is that understood?"

"Yes, miss. Thank you. You won't regret this."

"You're welcome. Now, forget about work and try to have a good time."

"Yes, miss." Footsteps hurried away, then faded within the noise of the room.

Ernst rubbed the back of his neck. Ilsa had taken the blame for her late report rather than tell him about the misdeed of her employees. Unsurprisingly, she was gracious and compassionate. The women had committed a terrible offense, yet she knew they needed the income from their jobs, and she was willing to give them a second chance. Would he have been so charitable? Probably not, but after seeing how she handled the situation, he would act differently in the future. He would become a man who deserved a woman like her.

Chapter Eighteen

Couples whirled around the floor, the rainbow of women's dresses brightening the room like a spring garden. Conversation and laughter mingled with the strains of the orchestra, and the chocolatey aroma of black forest cookies melded with the cinnamon and apple fragrance of the fritters. Ernst's mouth watered, and he glanced over his shoulder at the dessert table spread with a mixture of traditional German foods and American treats. A bowl of *Gebrannte Mandeln* caught his eye, and he spooned several of the candied almonds onto a small plate.

His gaze slid toward Ilsa who watched the dancers, her arms wrapped around her middle and her eyes clouded. Was she still cogitating about the conversation with her staff? Did she regret her decision to let the matter lie? Or was something else bothering her?

Mr. Orbison, one of Mr. Beck's newest hires, approached Ilsa and bowed. He said something Ernst couldn't hear, then she shook her head as she responded. The man's face fell. He replied, his words again too soft to hear, then pivoted and walked away.

Had he asked her to dance? Ernst popped the last of the coated nuts into his mouth, their sugary flavor exploding on his tongue. A favorite since he was a child, the delicacy brought back happy memories of sneaking the confection from the cooling racks on the kitchen table, his mother pretending not to notice. He smiled and wiped his sticky fingers on a napkin. He'd stalled long enough.

He poured two cups of punch, then took a deep breath and sauntered to Ilsa's side. Her face lit up at his appearance, and his chest puffed out. She seemed happy to see him, a definite plus after her rejection of Mr. Orbison. He handed her the glass cup, then clinked his vessel with hers. "Cheers." He took a long drink, the cool liquid soothing his parched throat. "Have you had fun tonight? You wouldn't have come if the attendance wasn't mandated."

"And I would have missed out. It's been a lovely evening." She made a vague gesture toward the crowd. "I've had a chance to get acquainted with lots of people, some of whom I've never seen. I forget how large the facility is and how many employees work for Mr. Beck."

"I'm glad you've enjoyed yourself." He smiled. "The size can be overwhelming, and the factory will probably get larger. At my level, I haven't seen the final plans, but Mr. Beck has indicated business is booming, and the company may require expanding."

"Already? That seems ambitious."

"Hardly." Ernst raised one eyebrow. "Perhaps he's become successful sooner than he anticipated, but I'm sure he planned to grow long before the first shovelful of dirt was dug. He's a savvy businessman."

"And I'm just a farm girl who wouldn't understand?"

"You're putting words in my mouth."

"True. I'm sorry." She fiddled with her cup. "Sometimes I wish for simpler times. I admire Mr. Beck and all he's done, even if it did anger Papa."

"The company has helped the community flourish. Why was your father set against Mr. Beck?"

She shrugged. "Papa didn't like change, especially change that wasn't his idea. He stuck to the old ways. Tobias has done a lot to modernize the farm. I often wonder if Papa would be proud or upset."

"It's a new era. Machinery and factories are the future."

"Yes, but the old ways aren't all bad."

"Agreed." He cocked his head. "Will you stay on board after your debt is repaid?"

"I haven't decided. I enjoy my new responsibilities, and I'm learning a great deal, more than I ever thought possible."

Ernst hesitated, then cleared his throat. "About your job... I overheard your conversation with the two girls who apologized for tearing up your report. I didn't eavesdrop intentionally...well, not at first, but then when I realized what they were talking about...anyway, you handled the situation well. Better than I would have."

Her cheeks pinked, and she waved her hand in a dismissive gesture. "It was nothing. They seemed genuinely contrite, although I don't understand why they would do such a thing. The girls said it was a dare, but what kind of employee does that?" She narrowed her eyes. "You don't think I should have recommended they be let go?"

"No. They seemed grateful enough to behave properly from here on out, but they do bear watching. You were right to tell them about regaining your trust." He rocked on his heels. "And I, um, owe you an apology for jumping to conclusions and admonishing you for no reason, as it turns out."

"The report was late. You had every right to scold me."

"Not a mistake I plan to repeat in the future, with you or anyone else. I'll conduct my due diligence first. A lesson learned for me, and I have you to thank for it."

She gave him a saucy smile. "Happy to help."

His heart flipped, and he swallowed as the orchestra began to play a waltz. "Enough conversation. May I have this dance? I believe it's the last of the night."

Setting her cup on the table, she curtsied. "Then by all means, we must participate."

He put down his cup beside hers, then grasped her hand in his, her skin soft and warm and led her among the other couples. She rested her palm on his shoulder, her petite frame fitting perfectly in his arms. The faint fragrance of lavender clung to her, and her hair smelled of soap. He was the luckiest man in the room. They danced as one, their steps and motions in flawless sync. Did he dare hope she could see how perfect they were for each other?

"Ilsa." He put his lips close to her ear. "I was a fool to let you go, and I'm sorry for the pain I caused you. Would you let me call on you again? Let me spend time with you to prove how much I care?"

She gaped at him, her eyes shooting blue sparks. "Why would you ask such a thing?"

"Uh, we are getting along so well." His mouth dried. "We had something special, and I ruined it. I can't change the past, but the future is ours for the grabbing."

"It's impossible." She tensed in his arms. "Female managers have enough trouble being taken seriously, and I'm under considerable scrutiny because of perceived favoritism from you."

"But—"

"If we court, everyone will believe something has been going on between us from the beginning. I can't allow that. I need my job. And my reputation."

"That's silly."

"What?" Her voice held a steel edge. "How dare you say that? Evidence you don't care for me as you claim. You belittle my opinion."

"No, I meant, well, we can't help what people think." He frowned. "We know the truth. Mr. Beck knows. No one else matters."

"Easy for you to say from your lofty position."

He dropped her hand. "You want to throw away a chance at happiness because of rumors and speculation?"

Uncertainty clouded her eyes, then she straightened her spine. "I can't. I'm sorry. It's too late." She turned away, then shoved her way through the dancers. She hurried to the door, grabbing her cloak from the hook on the way.

Ernst drew a shuddering breath. He had to stop her. "Ilsa, wait!" He bumped into several couples, apologizing as he made his way off the floor, then to the door. He ran outside as Ilsa climbed into her family's wagon, Tobias holding the traces. "Wait. I must speak to you."

Head bowed, she shook her head and murmured to Tobias, who glared at him. "I told you what I'd do to you if you hurt her."

"It's not his fault, Tobias." Ilsa laid her hand on her brother's arm. "It's mine. Let's go home."

"Ilsa." Ernst held out his hands.

Without turning, she said, "There's nothing to discuss, Ernst. I'm sorry I can't give you what you want."

Tobias slapped the horse's rump with the reins, and the wagon lurched forward, taking Ernst's broken heart with it.

Chapter Nineteen

Murky sunlight seeped through the drapes as Ilsa finished dressing. She buttoned her boots, then brushed her hair and plaited it. Sluggish after two restless nights with little sleep, she glared at her reflection in the mirror. She'd stayed home from church yesterday, then reprimanded herself for being a coward. Ernst would not have made a scene, but she couldn't face the look of disappointment she knew would be clouding his eyes.

She huffed out a loud breath. Would she see him today or would he make himself scarce? They'd have to interact at some point.

Before she'd run out, the Oktoberfest event had been delightful. She'd eaten too much of the delicious food, talked until she was hoarse, and danced intermittently. Interacting with her colleagues out of their work clothes in the party atmosphere had helped her see them in a new way. She'd learned that Mr. Davis liked to fish, and Miss Branche was an avid quilter. Two of the other new managers loved to read, and the three of them had discussed their favorite authors at great length. She smiled as she glanced at the stack of books on her nightstand. A stack that promised to grow after hearing about the latest publications.

Her parents had done little entertaining, but she'd attended church socials over the years. Somehow, Mr. Beck's party was different. Or was she different? Grown up now. Too bad Nadine or Tobias couldn't have come. They would have enjoyed getting off the farm.

A knock sounded. "Ilsa? Breakfast is ready." Nadine's voice was muffled. "Tobias has to go into town and said he'd take you to work."

"Coming." She opened the door. "Will he bring me home this evening, or should we put my bicycle in the back of the wagon."

"He'll come back for you."

"Wonderful." Ilsa grabbed her coat and pocketbook from a hook by the door. "I'm famished. What did you make?"

Their heels banged on the wooden steps as they descended to the empty kitchen. "Scrambled eggs, sausage, and biscuits. The men have already headed to work. Some sort of early meeting."

Ilsa's mind raced. Was she supposed to attend? No, she would have received notification.

"Are you all right?" Nadine peered at her. "Still feeling poorly?"

"I'm fine." Her faced warmed. "I, uh, wasn't as ill yesterday as I led you to believe. I skipped church to avoid Ernst."

Nadine pulled her into a quick hug, then released her and gestured to one of the vacant chairs. "Sit. I'll get your food."

Sinking in the chair, Ilsa waited in silence while her sister filled a plate, then set it in front of her. Her mouth watered at the tantalizing aromas emanating from the meal.

"First of all, you needn't have bothered. Ernst didn't show up either." Nadine grinned as she sat next to Ilsa. "Tobias told me the two of you seemed to have had some sort of argument, and I understand you stopped our little brother from jumping out of the wagon to pummel him."

With a giggle, Ilsa nodded. "Always ready to defend us, isn't he?" She sobered. "But it was my fault."

"What happened?" Nadine bolted upright. "Did you say something you shouldn't have?"

Ilsa sent Nadine a wry smile. "You mean like I often do?"

Nadine looked sheepish. "I meant—"

"We both know my mouth gets me in trouble." She patted her sister's arm. "Anyway, no, Ernst asked if he could come calling, and I turned him down." Ilsa slumped in the chair. "I'm an idiot, and I hurt his feelings."

"You turned him down?" Nadine's voice rose to a screech. "Why on earth would you do that? I thought the goal was to catch his eye."

"It was, then I panicked. Rumors are swirling that he is showing me favoritism because of our past." Ilsa frowned. "That we are more than colleagues. If I let him court me, people will believe the lies. I need to be taken seriously as an employee and a manager."

"You're choosing your job over happiness?"

Tears pricked the backs of Ilsa's eyes. "Ernst asked me the same question. I need this job. We have to pay off Papa's debt. It would be selfish of me to allow my personal life to overshadow that fact."

"You could get another job."

"Where? I'm not qualified for anything else other than farm work. Besides, if we did court and then marry, I'd have to resign anyway. Married women don't work." She shoved aside her empty plate. "Why is society so full of rules for women, dictating what we can and cannot do? I'm beginning to understand Mrs. Beck's suffragist leanings."

Nadine gasped. "You wouldn't join them, would you?"

"No, I can't risk my job. She has enough money that no one dares to criticize her stance, but being a lowly first-level manager..."

"But if Mrs. Beck is part of them, surely women at her husband's company wouldn't be adversely treated."

"Things are different for the rich, Nadine. I've seen it with my own eyes. The higher level managers who are making big salaries can do whatever they want. Those of us on the floor are held to a separate standard. I guess that's the way of the world."

"How unfair." Nadine cocked her head. "Did you discuss your job with Ernst? Maybe he could ask Mr. Beck to allow you to continue working."

"We didn't get that far before I, um, left." Ilsa sighed and ran her finger along a scar on the wooden tabletop.

""He followed you out." That's a good sign!" Nadine nudged Ilsa's shoulder. "He obviously loves you and wanted to make things right."

"I—"

"I've seen how he looks at you. Trust me when I say he is a man smitten."

"Even if that's the case, I can't ask him to take on my problems...our debt." Ilsa crossed her arms. "I won't do it."

"I understand how you feel, but instead of turning him down flat, you could ask him to wait until after we're done paying off the creditors. Did you consider that option?"

"No." Ilsa squirmed, and her heart thudded. "What if it's too late?"

##

Hunched over paperwork at his desk, Ernst rubbed his throbbing forehead. He'd been staring at the columns of numbers since lunch, and the digits had begun to blur. Normally excited by the process of compiling company statistics, he struggled to focus, instead continuing to revisit the memory of Saturday night's Oktoberfest. He'd enjoyed getting to know his coworkers in the collegial environment, the atmosphere creating a camaraderie as they explored similar interests. The food had been delicious, and he'd sampled several German dishes he hadn't eaten since childhood. The tastes brought back images of his grandmother puttering in the kitchen, making her own grandmother's recipes that had been handed down: the dog-eared, soiled pages of her collection bringing a smile to Grandmama's face and a song to her lips.

One to never meet a stranger, she would have enjoyed the festivities, ensuring she spoke to each and every guest, a trait that had embarrassed his reticent father as a child. Yet, the man had married a woman almost as gregarious. Ernst grinned. His mother went out of her way to greet others and had an uncanny ability to set even the most prickly person at ease. She, too, would have liked the party. Perhaps he could convince Mr. Beck to hold some sort of celebration for employees' family members, giving them a chance to see where their siblings, spouses, and children worked. His mother and Mrs. Beck would get on like long-lost sisters.

Ilsa's image from Saturday floated to his mind, and his pulse raced. She'd looked gorgeous, hardly the same girl he knew in high school. The teal hue of the dress had accentuated her crystal-green eyes, and her thick ash-blonde hair had glistened. They'd chatted like the old friends they were and laughed at shared memories. It had seemed that she'd shed the last of her anger at him for hurting her. They'd danced three times. His lips twisted. The last dance hardly counted because she'd stormed out halfway through. How could he have read her wrong? She'd seemed so forgiving, so inviting. Then he'd blurted out the request to renew their relationship. To come calling...code for courting. Oh, to take back the words.

He blinked and palmed his eyes, then glanced at the ledger. Still fuzzy. Time for a break. He rotated his neck to ease the stiffness, then massaged his shoulders. Rising, he closed the books, tucked them in his desk, and locked the drawer. He'd take a turn around the factory. Did he dare stop in the wrapping department?

Mr. Oxford, Beck's second-in-command, appeared in the doorway. "Afternoon, Webber. Mr. Beck would like to see you."

Ernst's eyes widened, and perspiration sprang out on his upper lip. "Me?"

The man winked. "Don't worry. You're not in trouble. He's been checking with all of us managers to get our opinion about Saturday's gala. Take your time. I just sent Mr. Corrigan up."

Pulse returning to normal, Ernst nodded. "Sure. Thanks for the heads-up."

"Say, you danced with your fair share of lovelies. Guess you had fun."

"You took quite a few turns around the floor." Ernst swatted the man's arm. "You were hardly abandoned."

Oxford guffawed. "True, but you waltzed with the prettiest girl in the room. One of the smartest, too. You're the envy of many."

"We're childhood friends. Nothing more." Ernst straightened his jacket and swallowed a sigh. "There's no need to start any rumors."

The man pinched his mouth between his finger and thumb. "You've got nothing to worry about from me. I know how to button my lips. Mr. Beck frowns on gossip, and I have no taste for it either."

Ernst clapped him on the shoulder as he walked past. "Thanks, Nigel. Sorry if I overreacted."

"No apology necessary. One can never be too careful."

Hurrying down the hall, Ernst looked neither left nor right. Mr. Oxford may have said he could take his time, but he wouldn't risk keeping the founder waiting. Breathless, he arrived outside the suite of offices where Mr. Beck conducted business as Mr. Corrigan exited. Knocking on the doorframe, Ernst peeked into the room. "You asked to see me, sir?"

Mr. Beck wore a broad smile. "Right on time, Webber. I won't keep you long, but I wanted to get your honest impression of our little party on Saturday."

"A rousing success." Ernst shifted in the upholstered chair. "People enjoyed themselves tremendously. I heard numerous compliments about the food and music, and two of the ladies specifically mentioned the décor. Folks were pleased to have an opportunity to wear traditional garb, some of it handed down from ancestors."

"Excellent." Mr. Beck leaned forward, propped his elbows on the desk, and steepled his fingers. "And how about you?"

"Me?"

"Yes. Did you have a good time, or was it a tedious company event?"

"Not at all, sir." Ernst rubbed his stomach. "I've rarely eaten such delicious food, and I liked getting to know my colleagues outside of work. I've discovered commonalities with some of them."

"And the dancing?"

"Very nice."

"Nice?" Mr. Beck raised one eyebrow and crossed his arms. "You danced with Miss Krause a few times, and unless I miss my guess, you thought it was more than nice. She's an excellent choice."

Ernst's jaw slacked. He should have realized Mr. Beck would keep an eagle eye on who interacted with whom and for how long. "I've told you that we're friends from high school, although I will admit she looked lovely."

"Friends, hmm. Nothing more?"

"No. She made her feelings quite clear."

"Ah, so you are interested in our up-and-coming gal." Mr. Beck winked. "The best marriages begin with a solid friendship."

"She refused me, sir. I asked to call on her, and she said no."

"You're giving up?"

"What choice do I have?"

"The choice to pursue her. If you truly feel you cannot live without this woman, then do something about it. Don't be inappropriate, but make opportunities to see her and be indispensable to her. Make her feel special."

"But she won't see me."

Mr. Beck frowned. "Use your head, man. Make your interactions here mean something. Again, don't cross the line of unprofessionalism, but tell her what you appreciate about her performance. You attend the same church. Be solicitous, but not overbearing. Ask her opinion on the sermon, that sort of thing. The town is growing, but not so large that you can't run into each other. Determine her habits and haunts. You're a bright young man. I have faith in you."

"You seem so sure this will work."

"Given enough time, I believe you will win her hand. But be patient. A woman's heart is a fragile thing."

"Did you have to be patient with Mrs. Beck, sir?" Ernst gulped. A bold question to ask the man. "Never mind, sir. I shouldn't have pried."

"Nonsense. I'm prying into your life. You have the right to pry into mine." Mr. Beck chuckled. "And yes, I had to be *very* patient. She turned me down a half-dozen times."

"Goodness! Uh, congratulations." Was Mr. Beck right? Did he have a second chance with Ilsa? His pulse sped up. He wouldn't know until he tried. And he would try. He'd work harder than he'd ever done.

Chapter Twenty

Ernst slipped into his wool overcoat, then clamped his homburg onto his head. He took one last glance around the office to ensure he'd stowed his paperwork and reports into his desk, then closed the door. He forced himself not to rush down the corridor and out of the building to where the wagon waited.

Three days had passed since his conversation with Mr. Beck. Three days during which he'd prayed, planned, and plotted about ways to spend time with Ilsa. He'd avoided her, and yesterday when he caught sight of her heading into the women's break room, she sent him a cautious glance. Apparently, Saturday night was still in her thoughts as well.

Mr. Beck must be playing matchmaker. Yesterday, the man had sent a memo to Ernst tasking him with taking the first-level managers on a tour of the town and explaining the upcoming changes and additions. The group would include Ilsa. Swallowing a smile, he shrugged. He'd accept any and all help wooing her.

His pulse quickened, and he shook his head. He'd spent an inordinate amount of time getting dressed this morning, donning and removing several suits before finally settling on the charcoal-colored jacket and slacks with a black herringbone vest. Not that he was superstitious, but he'd worn the outfit during the interview that had secured his job. Perhaps, it would go a long way to impressing the woman he hoped to marry.

"Stop it, man. You're putting the cart before the horse."

"Excuse me, sir?" A man approaching from the end of the hall looked startled. "Are you speaking to me?"

Face warm, Ernst shook his head. "Carry on." Great. The man would think him a ninny. Or mad. Or both. He pushed open the door and squinted against the glare. Unseasonably warm for October in Wisconsin, the morning had dawned bright and sunny under a cloudless blue sky, and remained summerlike throughout the day. Dressed in red, orange, and gold foliage, the trees appeared to be on fire in the late afternoon rays. Even the wilting grass had perked up.

A dozen expectant men and women gazed at him from the back of the wagon. He waved, then climbed onto the bench seat beside the driver and sat facing the managers. His gaze swept the group, his eyes resting on Ilsa a fraction too long. "I'm thrilled Mr. Beck asked me to be your guide, and I hope you'll be as excited as I am about his vision for the future Beck's and Cocoaville."

He nudged the driver. "Ready." The wagon lurched forward, then slowly wended its way down the lane, the horses' hooves clomping on the hard-packed ground. Ernst's body swayed with the rhythm of the conveyance. They rode in silence for several minutes until they reached the top of the rise behind the factory. He held up his hand, and the driver reined in the horses. Snorting, the animals arched their necks as if irritated they'd been asked to stop. Perhaps they were enjoying the excursion as well.

With a broad motion, he gestured toward the undulating meadows that stretched toward the trees. "The next phase of growth of the town will take place here and be geared toward the families of Beck Enterprises. At this time, there are plenty of shops in which to purchase your food, supplies, and household goods. The hospital is nearly complete, and the staff will be arriving by the end of the month. You will no longer have to travel into Green Bay or the other cities to obtain medical care. The lending library opens next week, and Mr. Beck has purchased books from all over the country. He has also secured subscriptions to the most popular magazines and other periodicals, so rather than purchase *Godey's Lady's Book* or *Harper's Weekly*, you will be able to borrow them for a period of time, thus saving you money."

One of the women sighed. "How very generous. I've not been able to afford *Godey's*." Several of the men nodded.

Ernst's chest puffed out. These folks recognized what Mr. Beck was doing for them, and happy employees made the best company ambassadors.

Pointing to the left, Ernst said, "Mr. Beck recognizes the importance of large, clean areas where children can play and socialize. Basing it on the sand gardens of his home country of Germany, he's calling it a playground."

"Sand gardens?" One of the men cocked his head. "I'm not familiar with those."

"I'm not sure when they originated, but the Germans created places for the city children to go so they didn't have to play in the streets. The areas held large expanses with piles of sand, and the kiddies were supervised by police officers. The idea was brought to Boston about twelve years ago by Dr. Marie Zakrzewska, a colleague of Dr. Elizabeth Blackwell. Mr. Beck is building on the concept, and the area will encompass a park with walking trails and gardens, as well as baseball fields with associated equipment, swings, seesaws, and ladders. He will be digging a pond so the children can canoe, but that won't happen until next summer."

"Impressive," Mr. Nader said.

"Over there will be an amusement park." Ernst motioned to the right. "Mr. and Mrs. Beck attended the Columbian Exhibition in Chicago four years ago and hope to create something similar on a much smaller scale. There will be a Ferris wheel and various rides. Construction will begin next summer as well, but may take some time to finish."

"Excuse me, but don't you think that's a waste of money?" Miss Branche, the newest manager in the labeling the department raised her hand. "And dangerous?"

A murmur rose from the others in the wagon.

Ernst peeked at Ilsa to gauge her reaction, but her face remained impassive. He looked at Miss Branche. "To answer your second question first, Mr. Beck will ensure complete safety of any and all rides. He would not put his employees or their families at risk." Ernst tapped his chin. "As to that it's a waste of money, I respectfully disagree. He understands the importance of providing for you, but he wants to do more than simply give you a fair wage. He recognizes that being able to spend money for an amusement park visit is a luxury most cannot afford."

"Is he trying to purchase our loyalty?" One of the women in the back narrowed her eyes at him. "Does he think these luxuries, as you call them, will ensure our happiness? Is he doing this to thwart the union attempts?"

"Not at all." Ernst shook his head. "Things never buy happiness, but before he started the company, he visited many facilities around Europe and the United States. He saw many company towns that held employees hostage, in a sense. They were given credit at company stores rather than wages. They could only rent their homes; homes that were barely livable and cramped together. Once an employee left the company, they were evicted. Mr. Beck was given a hand up during his early beginnings as a businessman. He wants to do the same for his employees, and frankly, he'd rather do it without outside interference such as unions."

Mr. Johnstone turned to Ernst. "That's why he allows us to purchase our homes, right?"

"Correct," Ernst said as Ilsa smiled at him. Encouraged, he continued, "Mr. Beck doesn't want you to live in poverty. He did that as a child and knows the debilitating effects of extreme need and hunger." Ernst signaled the driver, and the wagon began to move. "We'll be taking each of you home, and I'll point out other additions along the way."

A flock of crows swooped overhead, their raucous cries splitting the air as the vehicle lumbered toward town. When they reached the edge, Ernst pointed to a flat expanse. "Here is where the orphanage will be built. Never blessed with children of their own, the Becks have felt a need to create a place for local orphans, and this land will be enough to construct several small homes where some number of children and a set of house parents will live."

Ilsa beamed at him. "Individual homes? How innovative."

Ernst's pulse thrummed at her gaze. "Yes. Mr. Beck does his homework, and he read many studies that indicate children raised in homes flourished better than those who lived in a dormitory setting."

"You mentioned local orphans." Ilsa's brow wrinkled. "Are there many?"

"More than you'd think." Ernst nodded. "Mr. Beck had me contact facilities around the state, and at last count there were nearly two dozen who'd lived within thirty miles of here."

"Sad." A shimmer of tears glistened in her eyes.

"Yes. Until coming here, I took for granted the privileges I had while growing up."

One by one the passengers were dropped off at their houses until Ilsa and the woman who lived at the farm abutting hers remained in the wagon. He swung his legs around so he was facing forward as they chatted quietly. The group had appreciated the tour, and the information gave them food for thought. The union had only been brought up once, and he hoped he'd deflected the comment with grace. Unions had their place in companies where owners treated employees like chattel, but Mr. Beck truly cared for his staff. He didn't need an organization directing from behind. Ilsa's posture had changed from stiff to relaxed as time passed, finally bestowing her dazzling smile on him at the end. Dare he hope she'd forgiven him again?

The wagon stopped in front of her house, and he jumped down to give her a hand with getting out. She looked startled as he followed her to the door. "A moment alone, Ilsa? I won't keep you long."

She nodded.

He licked his lips and stuffed his hands into his pockets. "I wanted to let you know that I can ask for a transfer to a different department that would ensure we wouldn't interact. You'd submit your reports to someone else and get work direction from others."

"You like your job. Why would you do that?"

"To make you more comfortable and to cease any and all speculation about favoritism on my part."

"You said we can't help what people think."

"True, but—"

"No." She laid her hand on his arm. "I can't let you do that. It wouldn't be fair to you, and the move might be bad for your career."

"You are more important than any job. A lesson I learned the hard way by losing you, and we may never recover what we had, but that's of no consequence. I want to do what is right."

"I—"

"Don't give me an answer now. Think about it and tell me next week." He gave in to his desire and stroked her cheek, her skin soft under his fingers. "And don't feel any pressure. I am happy at Beck's no matter where I'm assigned."

Her eyes widened, and she nodded. "All right. Thank you for the offer."

Before he could do something stupid like kissing her, he whirled around and hurried to the wagon, his heart thundering in his chest. She hadn't slapped him for touching her. Was that a good sign? *Dear Lord, give me patience.*

Chapter Twenty-One

Hand to her face where Ernst had caressed her, Ilsa watched the wagon buck and sway as it headed toward the road. Miss Branche, who lived on the neighboring farm, waved and beamed at her, but Ernst sat ramrod straight, never turning to look. After several moments, the conveyance disappeared around the bend, but she remained on the porch.

Streaks of pink and purple materialized, and the sun dipped behind the trees, its orange rays casting shadows through the branches. A light breeze rifled her hair, and she shivered. Would winter arrive early this year? How many days before she'd have to exchange her bicycle for snowshoes to go to work?

With the moon absent in its new-moon phase, pinpricks of light dotted the deepening sky. She searched the expanse, recognizing the constellations Papa had taught her. He loved the pictures made by the stars and passed that fascination on to her. She traced her finger along the dots that made up Ursa Major, then down toward Leo, a collection of stars that looked nothing like a lion. She smiled at the memory of Papa urging her to use her imagination to see the outline.

Her favorite was Gemini, and she studied the heavens until she found the faint assembly of lights forming the two stick figures holding hands. Papa had warned her that some people put credence in the relationship between the stars and destiny, consulting the stars for guidance in their personal lives. Newspapers printed copious articles touting the science of what they called zodiac signs. Sad that readers sought the help from the creation rather than the Creator.

Her heart clenched. As she should have been doing about Ernst. Instead, she'd allowed her emotions to determine her response. Not that she should discount how she felt, but seeking God to make important decisions was something else Papa had taught her. To pray without ceasing. They'd talked long about that concept. She'd been twelve or thirteen when she stumbled on the phrase while reading her Bible. She tried to understand how she could go about her daily business while constantly praying. She'd wondered if the Apostle Paul who wrote the words meant she was supposed to pray instead of getting things done.

Papa had chuckled when she'd asked, but he wasn't making fun of her. He said he'd had the very same confusion when he first read the passage. He explained how the Bible wanted people to have an *attitude* of prayer, a continual dependence on God, talking to him about anything and everything. And she'd failed to do that.

First, she was angry at Papa for dying, then God for taking him. By the time she finally accepted that her parents were gone, she was working long hours at the factory, spending time on the road to and from the facility, and helping on the farm every chance she got. She'd permitted life to get in the way of living.

Forgive me, Father. Help me be wise and follow You. What would You have me do about Ernst? Is he the man You have chosen for me? Am I to marry, or does my future lie with providing an income for Nadine and Tobias? I care for Ernst too much and could easily fall in love with him again, but I will walk away if that is Your will.

She swallowed against the lump in her throat. Turning her back on Ernst might be the hardest thing she'd ever do, but today was a new day, and she would live as God commanded her. After all, He had her best interests in mind. Did that include remaining a spinster all her life? What did His plans entail?

A noise sounded from the side of the house, and she froze. She'd been cogitating for so long, she didn't notice that night had fallen. Had a cougar or wolf wandered onto the farm in hope of an easy meal? Perspiration pooled under her arms. Trembling, she crept to the edge of the porch and peered around the wall, then gasped at the tall, shadowy form.

"Ilsa." Tobias's voice broke the silence. "I thought you'd be inside by now. The temperature is dropping."

Her heart rate slowed to normal, and she licked her dry lips. Of course it was Tobias. Her fear had been foolish. They hadn't seen a wolf or big cat on the farm in years. And with Mr. Beck's town sprawling farther and farther, the wilderness was shrinking, pushing away the wild animals.

Wrapping her arms around her middle, she frowned. "You think I am too delicate to be outside? How many times have I trudged to the barn in the snow and ice? Helped harvest late into the evening when the frost was forming as we worked?"

He jogged up the stairs. "Forgive me." His teeth flashed in the light from the window. "You're as tough as nails."

She giggled and wagged her finger at him. "And don't you forget it."

"How could I with you around to remind me?" He opened the door and gestured for her to precede him.

As she stepped inside, he slipped off his boots, leaving them on the woven mat, then padded across the floor toward the kitchen. "I could use some coffee and food. How about you?"

"Sounds wonderful." She winked. "Just the thing to warm me."

With a chuckle, he shook his head and busied himself at the stove.

She cocked her head. "You're cooking? Where is everyone?"

"Nadine left the meal in the oven. Our boarders are working late, and she took the opportunity to attend the Ladies Guild. Did you want me to run you over there?"

"No, I've had enough people for one day." She sighed and sank into one of the ladderback chairs. "First work, then a tour with some of the other managers. I'm bushed." She pulled pins from her hair and ran her fingers through the tresses, then massaged her scalp.

After pouring two cups of steaming coffee and delivering them to the table, Tobias opened the oven and pulled out two bowls of fragrant beef stew. Her mouth watered as he put one in front of her, then sat across the table. With a smile, he reached for her hands, then bowed his head. She grasped his fingers, her heart full as she listened to him ask the blessing. When would she stop seeing him as her little brother and recognize the man he'd become?

He finished praying and released her hands. "Dig in. This has been simmering all afternoon."

Ilsa spooned a chunk of succulent meat into her mouth and moaned. No one cooked as well as her sister. She was truly gifted, making the most mundane dishes into delectable meals. Ilsa ate in silence, the memory of Ernst's last words floating into her mind.

"So, I heard your conversation with Ernst." He shrugged. "I didn't mean to eavesdrop."

She raised an eyebrow. "And?"

"And I think you should reconsider his offer."

"Ridiculous. You of all people know the pile of debt we're under. I can't do anything to jeopardize my job, and agreeing to let him ask for a transfer could do that. Mr. Beck is going to want to know why Ernst wants to move, and he won't lie about it. He's many things, but not a liar."

"From what you've told me, Mr. Beck is a reasonable man."

"But a tenacious and savvy businessman. I'm sure his company is more important to him than two people who want to court."

"So you do want to marry Ernst." Tobias ate another spoonful of stew. "Interesting."

"That's not what I said." She took a drink of water to collect her thoughts. "You're twisting my words."

"I've seen how you look at him when he's here. You still care."

"It's hard not to." She blew out a loud breath. "We had something special in high school. Yes, we were young, but our feelings were real. They were deep. We could talk about anything. We discussed our faith, exploring concepts in the Bible so we could understand them. We also talked about books we read. Our minds seemed to be as one." She waved her hand. "But I was obviously wrong if he was able to turn away so completely during college."

"Men can be fools, Ilsa. He was spreading his wings, trying new things. He let the glamor of being among intellectuals sway him. He sees the error of his ways."

"How would you know?"

"We talked one night after he brought the boarders home from work."

"But you threatened him at the Oktoberfest."

"I did. Well, actually a few days prior to that." Tobias played with his spoon. "Anyway, he needed to understand that I wouldn't allow him to get away with hurting you a second time. But his offer indicates he is putting you first in his life. As you should do for yourself."

She shook her head and ate the last remaining spoonfuls of stew, then dropped the utensil in the bowl with a clatter. "I can't put myself first, Tobias. We are a family, and family comes before anything. I have responsibilities, as do you. Would you run off with some girl instead of managing the farm?"

"For the right girl?" He smirked. "Absolutely."

"Ha. You're just saying that to make your point."

"Only partially. Not everything is as black and white as you make it. And nothing is forever, at least on this side of eternity. Instead of rejecting Ernst, ask him to wait for you. If he truly loves you, he will stand by you for as long as you need. Explain the situation and the responsibility you feel about seeing our repayment through to the end." He rose and came around the table, then sat in the chair next to her. Cradling her hands with one of his strong, calloused palms, he put the other arm around her shoulder. "You acted as our mother for a long time, but we're grown up. You don't have to be our mama any longer. We can be partners. All of us. The farm is doing well, even in the short time since you began working. The milk contract is generous, and the income from the boarders has already paid off more debt than we anticipated being able to do by now."

"But the Bible says to put others first."

"I'm no theologian, but I don't believe God expects you to do so to your own detriment." He rubbed her arm. "We are going to be fine, and it's going to take more time, but we will get to the other side and be debt free. I plan to purchase more cows and expand the farm. But I will also consider who I should court. I don't plan to be single forever, and neither should you."

"But—"

"Stop arguing, and listen to your heart. Talk to Ernst. He deserves to hear what you're thinking. And pray about the situation. God will close the door if He doesn't want you to walk through it." He tweaked her nose. "I handled dinner, so the dishes are yours. I'm headed to bed. Morning will be here early."

"Handled dinner?" She snorted a laugh. "All you did was pull it from the oven."

"Someone had to do the heavy lifting." He chuckled and sauntered from the room. "G'night, sis."

A smile tugging at her lips, she rose and cleared the table. His words were almost identical to those she'd told herself, yet she'd contested his as nonsense. She rolled her eyes. Had she always been this stubborn? Her smile broadened. Without a doubt. Could she change? Humble herself to reach out to Ernst? Follow God instead of marching forward expecting Him to keep up? *I'll do my best, Lord, but I can't do this without You.*

Chapter Twenty-Two

Ilsa signed her report and laid down her pen with a sigh. She collated the pages, then laid them in a neat stack on the corner of her desk. Her gaze went to the large clock at the far end of the room, and she smiled. Two hours early. She was getting more efficient with her work, and tasks took less time. During her first weeks as supervisor, she'd felt like a pig on roller skates, sure she'd made the biggest mistake of her life by applying for the job. When some of the girls had proved to be difficult and insubordinate, she'd second-guessed herself again, but the department now ran smooth and effectively.

She raised her head and surveyed the activity on the floor. Although concentrating on their work, the women seemed relaxed rather than frantic like when Mr. Davison had been their manager. He was a nice man, but his constant pacing between the machines and reminding them of their production quotas had created a frenzied environment.

Her style was different. She gathered her staff each Monday morning to explain their goals for the week, encourage them to do their best, and assure them she knew they could do they work. She'd also scheduled herself to operate the machines, and the women appreciated her working side by side with them. They'd exceeded their numbers every week since she'd started having the meetings.

Forgive my pride, Lord.

Zlata caught her eye and lifted her hand in a quick wave. The woman had been a gift. Always positive, she'd floated to the top of the group as a leader. She said she didn't want to be a supervisor, but she had the skills to be a good one. She was also one of the department's best wrappers. Her fingers were a blur as she worked her machine.

Ilsa smiled back at her, then turned her attention to Yasmina. They'd come to an uneasy truce, and two weeks had passed since she'd said or done anything to undermine Ilsa. Had she decided heckling her wasn't worth the effort, or was she biding her time to do something truly disruptive? Talk of unions had frittered away until only an occasional mention was made. Mr. Beck must be pleased, but how long before the thought of organizing revived? The topic had come up with the boarders at dinner last night, and they seemed optimistic that the employees had realized the unions would not improve their lot, and that Mr. Beck listened to their concerns, responding with amenable solutions.

Pulling the most recent issue of *The Commercial & Financial Chronicle* toward her, she perused the front page. Mr. Beck also ensured that his managers were knowledgeable about the latest business news by carrying several subscriptions to the periodical. At first, she'd found the journal dry and tedious, but then she began to compare the information to events in the weekly newspaper, and the correlations intrigued her. Now, she looked forward to *The Chronicle's* arrival.

Tobias teased her about her newfound interest, but the boarders seemed impressed. Not that she sought their admiration, but she appreciated being taken seriously, and she enjoyed the protracted discussions during evening meals. Would there ever be a time when women could rise through the ranks of companies, perhaps even running or owning a business? What an exciting day that would be.

An article about an international monetary conference and a debate about using silver versus gold as a standard took up several pages, and she made notes of her questions as she read. She bypassed a glowing account of a tribute to Commodore Vanderbilt and the statue being erected in Nashville in favor of a piece about the sale of the foreclosed Union Pacific Railway. Hard to believe that the once mighty railroad had financial troubles. Pages of stock results followed, and she skipped to the end to find the general investment news, her favorite section because she discovered many unknown companies buried between reports about railroads and mines.

"Ilsa?"

She whipped up her head and blinked, trying to focus on the two men standing next to the desk. Staring at the tiny print had blurred her vision. Cheeks warm, she rubbed her eyes. "Ern...I mean, Mr. Webber, how may I help you?"

"Miss Krause, this is Mr. Johnstone. I'm not sure if you had an opportunity to meet him at the Oktoberfest."

Rising to her feet, she extended her hand. "I haven't had the pleasure. Welcome to wrapping." She cocked her head, her gaze flicking from Ernst to Johnstone, then back again before she shot a glance at the clock. Still an hour before her report was due. Was he here for something else? Why bring the other man?

"Thank you, miss. I've heard nothing but glowing accounts about the efficiency of your department. I can't wait to work with you."

"Excuse me?" She narrowed her eyes at Ernst whose expression wavered between guilt and satisfaction, an odd combination. "I don't understand."

"I'll let Mr. Webber explain, but I'm here to collect your report if it's ready. If not, I can come back later."

She reached for the sheaf of papers and thrust them into his hand. Had Ernst come early to prove a point or to test her in some way? Was he trying to show he had no favorites? She pressed her lips together, then crossed her arms. He had quite a bit of explaining to do.

He had the grace to look uncomfortable, his eyes sending a silent plea to give him a chance. "Did I not tell you she was one of the best first-line supervisors we have?"

With a sigh, she sent him a tentative smile. Her temper had flared again, but fortunately she'd kept it contained and not said anything stupid or rude. When would she learn not to jump to the conclusion that Ernst was trying to annoy or discredit her? Nadine would tell her she was too sensitive for her own good, and her sister would be correct.

"Miss Krause, please join me." His lips curved, and he clapped Johnstone on the shoulder. "We'll return shortly. Remain here in case the ladies have any questions or problems, although you shouldn't have any issues."

The man put two fingers to his forehead in an exaggerated salute, then bowed to Ilsa. "If your staff is as well-trained as I've heard, I'll be a mere figurehead while you're gone." He gestured to the periodical. "Do you mind if I read your copy?"

Ilsa gaped at him. What was happening? "Um, sure. I'm finished, so you may take it with you."

"Excellent."

Ernst gestured for her to join him, and she nodded. They walked down the aisle, and she hesitated at the door. He shook his head. "It's a gorgeous day. Let's take a turn around the courtyard."

"All right." She tucked her hands into her pockets and wadded some of the fabric into her damp palms. What could he possibly want to discuss out of earshot of her staff?

Moments later, he pushed open the door that led to the patio area surrounded on three sides by knee-high brick walls. Tables and chairs took up most of the space, but several benches were lined up to face the grassy expanse behind the building. In the distance, the trees were nearly bereft of their colorful leaves. Winter would arrive soon, but today she'd enjoy the summerlike temperatures.

She lowered herself on the nearest bench, then crossed her ankles. Ernst paced in front of her, and a whiff of bay rum wafted past. Her toes curled, and she forced herself to pay attention.

"Thank you for seeing me." He stopped in front of her. "I'm sure this all seems quite clandestine, but I just wanted us to have some privacy. Noise from the machines make extended conversations a challenge." He tugged at his collar. "Anyway, I wanted to let you know that I requested a transfer, and Mr. Beck granted my petition."

"But I haven't given my answer."

"Even if you say no to courting, a transfer is a good business decision. If I want to progress within the company, I should know as much about the different departments as possible. Mr. Beck agreed the change was a good idea. In fact, he wants to revolve his managers through all the departments. He's calling it cross-training." Eyes sparkling, Ernst waved his hands as he talked. His excitement was palpable as he continued, "My first assignment is to create the system, taking into consideration how long each person should remain in place. If the moves are done too quickly, they could become disruptive. I start immediately, and Mr. Johnstone will be taking my place, but don't feel you have to rush your answer."

She tilted her head. He'd proved his integrity by handling the situation on his own, finding a solution that removed the burden of decision from her and benefited the company. Nadine was right. He had changed, or rather had gone back to being the selfless, generous man she'd known before college.

His gaze seemed to caress her, and her pulse quickened. "I don't need more time. I'd be honored to have you court me."

Ernst whooped and grabbed her hands. He pulled her to her feet, then wrapped his arms around her in a tight embrace.

Ilsa giggled, then extricated herself from his grasp, her cheeks scorching. "Behave yourself. The windows have eyes, and we must comport ourselves professionally. Our relationship is to be kept between us. I don't want others to know." His face fell, and she nibbled her lower lip. Her first act of their courtship was to hurt his feelings. Would he regret asking her?

Chapter Twenty-Three

Stepping back, Ernst wrapped his arms around his middle. How could he be so happy, yet disappointed at the same time? Ilsa was willing to court him, but only in secret. What kind of relationship was that? He watched myriad emotions play across her face, none of which was love.

He huffed out a breath and resumed pacing. He didn't remember her being so sensitive to what others thought about her. She hadn't been cavalier, but neither had she allowed others' opinions sway her behavior. If she knew what she was doing was right, she remained on course. What had happened while they were apart?

"Ernst." She reached for his arm, and he flinched. "Ernst, I'm sorry. Let's talk about this. Please. We used to be able to talk about anything."

He froze and scrubbed at his face with cold fingers. He'd judged her as sensitive, then pouted like a child at her request. "You're right." He motioned toward the bench. "I should apologize, not you. It's just that I'm thrilled you are willing to let me call on you, and I want to tell the world."

She sat down, fists clenched in her lap.

Lowering himself beside her, he patted her hands, then leaned on his thighs, his hands dangling between his knees. "Are you still unsure about us? Do you wish you'd not said yes?"

"No!" Her voice squeaked, and she cleared her throat. "No."

"Then what is it? Do you want to be able to get out of the relationship with no one the wiser if it doesn't work out?"

Her chin trembled.

"I'm trying to understand. Really, I am. I know you want to be taken seriously. I know you don't want any appearances of favoritism. I thought by agreeing to court, those concerns had faded. Am I wrong?"

"You're not wrong." She squeezed his arm. "I appreciate that you put in for the transfer, and it's wonderful that Mr. Beck saw this as a new way to operate his company. I love seeing you so enthusiastic about the new job, rather than merely accepting it as a means to an end." She rubbed her forehead. "But I'm trying to figure out how to juggle this."

"How can I help?"

Gratitude lit her face, and his chest swelled. "I'm rushing you, aren't I?"

"Not terribly. After all, I've said yes. You would think *I'd* want to tell the world."

He chuckled. "When the time is right. You are so good at your job that I forget you've only been working at Beck's for ten weeks. It's as if you've always been there. You've already received a promotion, and your department is one of the most productive."

She ducked her head.

"You didn't want to work for us, and now you can't imagine not."

"Is that perfectly awful?"

"Of course not." He gazed into the distance. "You've had a lot of upheaval in your life, painful as well as positive. You need time to adjust, and I'm plowing over you like a farmer with an out of control horse."

A shadow passed across her eyes.

"Should I not have said farmer?" He twisted his lips. "You miss your father."

Tears shimmered in her eyes, and she nodded. "My grief comes upon me when least expected. Mostly, I'm able to remember him with only a dull ache, then something, a sound or scent...or a word, brings reality crashing back. He is gone, and I am an orphan."

"I do not want to offer platitudes, but your heavenly Father is with you."

"Yes, but sometimes a human hug would be comforting." She swiped at her eyes, then straightened. "But I still have Nadine and Tobias close by, so I should count my blessings."

"Anytime you want a hug..." He wiggled his eyebrows.

She swatted him with a laugh. "Nice try, Mr. Webber."

His breath whooshed out. He'd chased away her sadness. "Just trying to do my part." He stretched out his legs. "In all seriousness, I'd like to know how to proceed. I will bow to your wishes, but I need to know what those are. How can we court if we're not to be seen in public?"

"Am I overreacting in my desire to conceal our relationship?"

With a grin, he said, "Will I get in trouble if I answer truthfully?"

"Hmm. Answering a question with a question. Sly." She smoothed her skirts and gave him a saucy smile. "All right. I admit I'm *unnecessarily concerned* about others finding out about us."

"A diplomatic way of putting things."

"Hey—"

He held up his hands. "As a man I can't understand your experiences because I haven't had them, but I can respect that the incidents have affected you. How about this: You will guide our pace. You will determine when and where we see each other. Our interactions at work will be minimal because of my new position, but we will see each other at church and its socials, and perhaps you will allow me to come to dinner occasionally. And my parents still haven't had you and your siblings to the house. A gross oversight, according to my mother."

"Sounds rather stringent."

His pulse thrummed, and he held his breath.

"But I think it's for the best. At least, initially."

He nodded, schooling his features so she wouldn't see his disappointment. From inside the building the muffled clang of the bell sounded, announcing break time. "We've been out here long enough.

"Thank you for being so accommodating. Most men would think I'm being silly."

"I hope you'll figure out that I'm not most men." He winked and tugged at a strand of her ash-blonde hair. "I've agreed to your terms, but I don't have to like them. I care for you, Ilsa, and I will show you how much, even within these parameters."

She blushed, and he swallowed a smile. If he wasn't mistaken, her feelings ran as deeply as his own.

Chapter Twenty-Four

The last strains of music faded, and the congregation seated itself. The rustle of skirts whispered and shoes scraped on the wooden floor. Ilsa peeked from the corner of her eye at Ernst seated next to her, his parents on his other side. His mother had enveloped her in a warm hug prior to the service and insisted the two families share a pew. Had the idea been hers or her son's?

He shifted, and his leg pressed against her thigh for a split second. His quick intake of breath matched hers, and she met his eyes. On her left, Nadine coughed quietly, and Ilsa whipped her head around. Her sister's eyebrow was raised nearly to her hairline. Her mouth was set in a slash, and she jerked her head toward the preacher.

Cheeks burning, Ilsa wrinkled her nose and turned toward the front of the church. Still aware of Ernst's form beside her, she forced her attention to the pastor, who had just finished reading a passage in John. *Forgive me, Lord.*

"Good morning, beloved." He beamed as he looked out over the crowd. "How are you feeling today? Tired? Sad? Content? Happy? How about joyous? Most people equate joy with happiness, but they are not the same thing. Happiness is fleeting, an emotion that ebbs and flows often based upon circumstances. Interestingly, the root of the term comes from the Old Norse word happ, meaning luck or chance. Joy is something you have in spite of your circumstances. Do you see where I'm going?"

Ilsa nibbled the inside of her cheek. It was as if Pastor Krueger had been watching her. Ever since Papa's death, she'd been riding a roller coaster; one minute being upset and the next feeling cheerful, her state of mind affected by whatever was happening at the time. She'd allowed herself to be buffeted by the seas of uncertainty.

"Your heavenly Father wants to give you an abundant life, more than simple happiness. He wants you to have joy. Let's read the Scripture again in John, chapter ten, verse ten: 'The thief cometh not, but for to steal, and to kill, and to destroy; I am come that they might have life, and that they might have it more abundantly.' The Greek word that is translated abundantly carried the concept of beyond that which is anticipated, excessive, exceedingly, or vehement. He will give you a life that passes the expected limit."

He pressed his hand against his chest. "I don't know about you, but I often take expectations into a situation. I rehearse in my mind what I think is going to happen, mulling over and over my anticipations. Sometimes those expectations come true. A lot of times they don't. Because I'm dealing with human beings. But God..." He grinned. "My favorite phrase from the Bible, folks...but God exceeds my expectations without fail. No matter what is happening to me physically, emotionally, or spiritually, God provides abundant life. That doesn't mean my life will be full of roses. We are part of a broken world, beloved, so we will experience pain. But God..." He pointed to the ceiling. "But God walks beside us, allowing us to be joyful despite our current condition."

Ilsa plucked at her skirt and blinked away the tears that welled in her eyes. Papa's death was hard, but good had come out of it. They'd been able to set up payment plans for his debt, the farm was thriving, and she had a job that she enjoyed and provided for them. The boarders were an added bonus, both in income as well as assistance for Tobias. She'd been so caught up in the difficulties, she'd missed the blessings.

Pastor Krueger closed his Bible and leaned on the podium. "Lots of changes have occurred and will continue into the foreseeable future, folks. Our little village has exploded in population. We don't know all of our neighbors, and we have to wait in line to make purchases. I could go through the litany of alterations that have entered our corner of the earth, but I won't. You are well aware of them. Some people find change to be scary. Others are excited by new possibilities."

Stroking the worn, leather-bound volume, he said, "I have good news for you. God never changes. Let me say that again. God. Never. Changes. And the closer your relationship with Him, the more joyous and abundant your life. 'Seek ye first the kingdom of God, and His righteousness, and all of these things will be added to you.' Matthew knew what he was talking about. He was a career tax collector, a vocation that brought wealth through corruption. By following the Master, he learned a *abundant* spiritual life greatly outweighed earthly *abundance*. Which would you rather have?"

His gaze, though gentle, pinned her to her seat, and Ilsa licked her lips. Others may have needed Pastor Krueger's sermon, but God had definitely wanted her to hear the man's words. Feeling both chastised and encouraged, she sighed and glanced at Ernst, who appeared as thoughtful as she felt. Apparently, the lesson had touched him, too.

She rose with the rest of the congregation to sing the final hymn, her mind racing as she mouthed the words. So much to think about, and she was eager to get started. She regularly read her Bible, but of late the exercise of morning devotions had become rote. No longer. She would dig in and study. Question and examine. Like she used to do. She and Ernst had debated passages and concepts during high school. What little they knew of life back then.

After the benediction, he grasped her elbow and leaned toward her, his breath tickling her cheek. "Nadine has invited my parents and me to lunch."

"Excellent." She smiled at him, and his face lit. Why had she waited to say yes?

##

The carriage ride from the church to Ilsa's family farm seem to take forever. Ernst jiggled his leg as he stared out the window at the passing countryside. The trees were nearly bare, and the grass had withered. Most of the fields were shorn, the stubble from cornstalks and other produce poking from the soil, but some were verdant with winter wheat. Other pastures were filled with meandering cows who grazed in the midday sun.

His mother laid her hand on his knee, and he sent her a sheepish smile as he stilled his leg. He returned his gaze to the view outside the window. They'd entered the lane that led to the Krause property. Finally. He tugged at his sleeves, willing his nerves to stop jumping. He'd known the family since he was in short pants. There was no need for anxiety. Yet, his pulse continued to skitter.

A corner of the house came into view, then disappeared behind the last rise. Moments later, the entire home emerged. The wraparound porch on the two-story abode held several rocking chairs. Flower beds at the base of the stairs had been cleaned out, the dark brown dirt contrasting with the whitewashed wood. The conveyance halted, and Ernst opened the door. He climbed out, then turned to take his mother's hand as she stepped down. His father followed, and they headed toward the house.

As they approached, the door swung wide, and Nadine waved from the threshold. "I'm so glad you could come. It's been too long."

"Thank you for inviting us." His mother ascended the stairs and looped her arm with Nadine's. "We should have had you over first. Shame on us."

"Nonsense." Nadine led them deeper into the house, her heels sharp on the wooden floors. "It's too soon since Papa's death for entertaining, but I've never been one to hold to society's directives. Besides, a casual Sunday lunch can hardly be equated with a ball or gala."

The dining table was covered with an embroidered cloth. Blue-and-white place settings were reminiscent of his mother's. Bowls were filled with steaming, fragrant dishes. Misters Corrigan and Nader waited by the sideboard next to Tobias, and Ilsa hurried into the room carrying a large platter on which a pork roast was nestled among root vegetables. Ernst's mouth watered as she put the salver in the center of the table, and he was struck again by the look of peace mingled with excitement on her face.

Nadine gestured for everyone to seat themselves, and Ernst found himself next to Mother on one side and Mr. Nader on the other. To his delight, Ilsa was directly across from him. When she looked up, he winked, and her face took on a delightful shade of pink.

After Tobias said the blessing, the food was passed, and Ernst's plate was soon piled high.

"You've outdone yourself, my dear." Mother beamed at Nadine. "I've never tasted such tender pork, and the seasoning is quite unusual."

"Thank you."

Mr. Corrigan nodded. "I count myself lucky to have been assigned to Miss Krause's house. I don't plan to go anywhere."

"I knew we made a wise decision in asking her to board our employees." Ernst chuckled and turned to the man. "So, you'll work for food? Mr. Beck can lower your salary?"

"Clever, Mr. Webber."

Tobias nudged Ilsa. "She is the best cook. Ilsa, here, can burn water. That's why we always have her handle outside chores."

"Hey—"

"That's all right, sis. You have other gifts, too." Tobias smirked. "Like telling people what to do." He glanced at Ernst. "I'll bet she's done well as a supervisor."

"You know I can hear you."

"He's just jealous of your success." Ernst's mother shot Tobias a smug look. "Don't worry. He'll get used to it eventually."

Ernst gaped at his mother, then threw back his head and laughed. Sass had never been her style, but it suited her. A glance at his father told him the man approved. "As a matter of fact, she is doing well. Her department is one of our highest performers. She knows when to be firm and when to allow them some leeway. She could teach some of our other managers a few techniques."

Ilsa swatted Tobias's arm. "What do you say now, *little* brother?"

He wiped his mouth on his napkin. "My apologies, sis. I stand corrected."

"It seems you're all doing well, Tobias." His father stabbed at a carrot. "I saw the size of your herd. And your fields look like they rendered a healthy harvest."

"Yes, sir. I'm pleased with the results of this season." Tobias gestured toward the boarders. "And these men are part of the reason. They come home from a long day of work and pitch in around the farm. Weekends, too. Having the extra help has been a real blessing."

Mr. Nader held up his hands. "I've earned these callouses fair and square. And I've learned a lot about running a farm. Enough to know I'll stick with manufacturing, thank you very much. Mr. Krause works harder than I ever will."

"Amen to that." Mr. Corrigan spoke around a mouthful of food. "I did my time in farming as a youngster. That's why I went to work in the factories."

"Kind words, gentlemen, but overstated." Tobias looked embarrassed. "Anyway, the farm still has room for growth. In fact, I hope to add more cows in the spring. I've been talking to Mr. Kemp about purchasing some of his heifers to increase my milk production."

"Really?" Ernst laid down his fork. "That's unexpected news." Was that what Ilsa was going to tell him?

"Well, the income from the boarders has allowed us to pay down more of the debt than planned, giving me some breathing room."

"Tobias," Ilsa hissed, her cheeks red. "I'm sure the Webbers are not interested in our financial woes."

"They're friends, Ilsa, almost family." He shrugged. "Mr. Kemp is going to let me pay in installments, freeing up cash for feed and improvements."

Nadine piped up, "And speaking of boarders, we're considering an addition to the house. For more boarders if they're available, Ernst."

"If the company expands as much as Mr. Beck hopes, we'll definitely need more lodging for the single employees. The married employees tend to want their own place."

"Speaking of marriage, Ernst, when were you going to ask me about courting Ilsa?"

Chapter Twenty-Five

Ernst swallowed, and a nervous laugh escaped. He couldn't tell from Tobias's expression if he was teasing or serious, and the wrong answer could spell disaster. "I, uh—"

An awkward silence blanketed the table as the diners exchanged glances.

"Leave him alone, Tobias." Ilsa looked down her nose at her brother. "I've only just agreed."

"He asked before coming to me?" Tobias cocked his head. "I would think that is the first step."

"You're right." Ernst finally found his voice. "I should have made an appointment. I'm sorry."

"Nonsense. I'm of age and a working professional. You do not need to seek my brother's approval. I'm quite capable of making the decision on my own." She poked Tobias. "Besides, I see the twinkle in your eye. You've made Ernst suffer long enough. Tell him you're joking."

Tobias clapped Ernst on the shoulder and laughed. "Sorry, old man. I couldn't resist. Congratulations. You've got your hands full with this one, but I wish you the best."

Ernst's breath exploded from his chest, and he sagged against the chair. "I've forgotten how brutal you can be with your pranks. You took at least a year off my life, friend."

Still chuckling, Tobias extended his arm, and Ernst grabbed his hand as Nadine squealed and jumped up. She skirted the table and ran to Ilsa, enveloping her in a hug. "You didn't tell me."

Everyone began talking at once, the meal forgotten. More congratulations rained down on them, and Ernst looked at his parents. He hadn't told his family either, but Mother's and Father's faces glowed. They didn't appear upset at having been left out.

When the hubbub had ceased, and Nadine returned to her seat, Ilsa held up her hands. "There is a reason we've not been forthcoming about this. I'd rather keep the information within family." She nodded to the boarders. "And I would appreciate if you gentlemen would keep this to yourself. As work colleagues, Ernst and I don't want our relationship to cause undue hardship. I hope you understand."

The men nodded in unison, and Mr. Nader said, "The news isn't ours to share, miss, but I don't see how such a happy occasion can cause problems."

Ernst's gaze slid toward Ilsa. How would she respond? She apparently hadn't planned to tell her family, but Tobias had guessed and let the proverbial cat out of the bag. How many others would figure out they were seeing each other? The two families sharing a pew had probably already started speculation. Trying to keep their courtship secret might be more challenging than she'd anticipated. He swallowed a grin. He wouldn't be disappointed should word get out.

"I appreciate your encouragement, Mr. Nader, but one must remain professional at all times, leaving one's personal life at the door. Mr. Webber and I don't want anything misconstrued and are merely taking precautions."

"As you wish, miss." The man nodded again but looked doubtful. He rose and bowed to Nadine. "Thank you for another delicious meal, Miss Krause. I'm working an extra shift tonight, so don't expect me for the evening meal."

"Me, too." Mr. Corrigan got up and touched his forehead. "Again, congratulations." They headed out of the room, and their footsteps faded.

Ernst pushed away his plate and tossed his napkin on the table. "How about if Ilsa and I do the dishes, Nadine?"

"Later. I've got coffee and cake that I thought we could enjoy in front of the fire in the parlor."

"Good idea." Tobias stacked Ernst's plate on his, then stood. "More time to quiz big sister."

"Not going to happen. We've discussed all we're going to about the subject." Ilsa grabbed two empty bowls. "Instead, we should create a plan to find a wife for Tobias and a husband for Nadine."

Nadine squeaked, and Tobias glared at Ilsa. "Touché, sis. How about if we talk about the latest letter from Heddie. We can share it with the Webbers."

Ernst's mother perked up. "We'd love to hear how she's doing. Such a lovely young woman."

"Perfect." Ilsa bobbed her head toward the doorway. "Make yourselves at home in the other room. Tobias will start the fire and join you while Ernst, Nadine, and I finish clearing."

His parents rose and followed Tobias as Ernst huffed out a breath. Even with the boarders gone, Ilsa didn't want to talk about their courtship. Was she flustered that the topic had come up unexpectedly, or was she unsure she wanted to pursue the relationship and the less said the better? She insisted she'd given the matter serious thought before saying yes, but her reticence to talk about it with family sent warning bells clanging in his head. Should he exercise patience or persistence?

Chapter Twenty-Six

Taking a sip of water, Ilsa looked at Ernst over her glass. A week had passed, and they were eating dinner with his parents, one of the few places they could be together without worrying about being seen. She set down the drinking vessel and frowned. She'd been praying day and night about the situation, but her noisy thoughts kept blocking the Lord's voice. She knew she was being foolish, but she couldn't seem to get out of her own way. Most girls would be over the moon to be with Ernst.

Thick sandy-brown hair and walnut-colored eyes that missed little, he had a dimple in his left cheek that appeared when he smiled or laughed. His square jaw was regal rather than haughty, and his figure, although not overly tall, was solid. She'd always felt safe in his embrace, his muscular arms firm and strong. He winked at her, then his gaze went to her lips, and her pulse sped up.

"Would you care for some more chicken, Ilsa?" Ernst's mother motioned to the platter in the middle of the table. "You've hardly eaten a thing."

Face burning, Ilsa whipped her head toward her. "No, ma'am. Everything was delicious. Nadine would love to have your recipe, I'm sure."

Mrs. Webber waved her hand in a dismissive gesture. "I doubt that, but you're very kind."

"She's always looking for new ways create meals, and I'm sure she'd want to know how you've made this after I tell her how good it is."

"Well, all right. Remind me before you leave." His mother sighed. "It's wonderful our families have reconnected. That *you* have reconnected. I can't tell you how disappointed we were when Ernst informed us that you two were no longer seeing each other. Such a mistake." She smiled and patted Ilsa's hand. "But that's been remedied."

"Mother." Ernst pinched the bridge of his nose. "We talked about this."

"Fine." She grinned at Ilsa. "But know that if Ernst hadn't come to his senses, I may have intervened. You are just what he needs. My son is entirely too serious and career-minded for his own good."

Ilsa nearly choked. If only the woman knew about the conversations she'd had with Ernst about her own career. "Uh, well, his job *is* important."

"Bah. Family is much more important."

"Enough, Frieda. Let the boy alone." Mr. Webber chuckled. "Can you tell us a bit about what you do, Ilsa? You seem to be getting on quite well, having already been promoted."

"I oversee first shift in the wrapping department. There are two dozen machines that do the actual work, but the girls must keep the hopper loaded with the colored foil and ensure the chocolates are covered correctly. They're to set aside any pieces that aren't perfect, but fortunately we have very few. My staff is very adept."

"How exciting to manage other people," Mrs. Webber gushed.

"Exciting is one word for it." Ilsa twisted her lips. "Challenging is more accurate."

Mr. Webber nodded. "Having managed people for most of my career, I agree wholeheartedly, but Ernst says you are very good, and your staff respects you."

"They seem to." She laid her napkin on the table. "I also work a machine for part of my shift each day. I enjoy the work, but it helps me know what the girls are experiencing."

"Very savvy, Ilsa." Mr. Webber tilted his head. "And how are you and your siblings getting along at home? It's only been a few months since your father passed. Are you coping?"

Her eyes welled, and Ilsa blinked away the moisture. "As well as can be expected. We stay busy and that helps. And it's not as if we're children and don't understand that people die."

"Yes, but you must allow yourselves to grieve. Losing one's parent is difficult no matter your age."

"And you must consider us your parents, now." Mrs. Webber dabbed at her eyes. "Not that we can take their place, but we can support and encourage you. All of you."

"That means a lot. I will tell Tobias and Nadine."

"When you're ready, we'd love to hear stories about your folks." Mr. Webber crossed his arms. "I found that reminiscing helped me when I lost my parents. Not right away, of course, but eventually. That and realizing that I would see them again in heaven."

Ilsa rubbed at the side of her glass. "I have been clinging to that very thing. I stumbled on several Bible verses recently, reminding me that our saying goodbye on earth isn't forever."

"But missing them is hard." Mr. Webber cleared his throat. "The hurt will never completely go away, but the pain will diminish to a dull ache. Frieda and I will be praying for you all."

"Thank you for speaking of them and of our loss." Ilsa's heart swelled. Ernst's parents were good people and had always treated her as family. She'd been foolish to turn her back on them after he'd spurned her. "People at church don't seem to know what to say. They avoid talking about Papa and Mama, as if they will make us upset by doing so."

Mr. Webber drained his glass. "Well, you can talk to us anytime."

"You boys head into the parlor." Mrs. Webber rose and began to collect plates. "Ilsa and I will bring the coffee and dessert. We can reminisce or simply enjoy the fire."

"Are you sure we can't help, Mother?"

"Leave the women to it, Ernst." Mr. Webber clapped Ernst on the shoulder. "You can try to build points with Ilsa another time."

Ilsa giggled and began to clear the table. "You get kudos for asking, Ernst."

He puffed out his chest and tucked his thumbs under his arms. "What do you think about that, Father?"

"I think a woman in love will say whatever she wants her man to hear." Mr. Webber grinned. "Come, son, we've got a fire to build." They tromped from the room, their laughter fading.

Ilsa's hands trembled. Was she in love? She followed Mrs. Webber into the kitchen, and they made quick work of preparing two trays, one with a pot of coffee and cups, the other with plates of delectable-looking apple strudel. Holding the drink tray, she headed toward the parlor.

"I love her so much, Father. Thank you for all your advice."

She gasped, and her steps faltered. He'd yet to declare his love to her. He'd said he cared, but that wasn't the same. Did he truly love her, or was he saying what he thought his father wanted to hear?

##

Ernst started as footfalls entered the room. Heart in his throat, he turned. Ilsa set a tray filled with a coffeepot and cups on the table in front of the sofa. Was she avoiding his eyes? Had she heard their conversation? His declaration of love? He hadn't use that word with her yet. Saying he cared had brought the look of a rabbit snared in a trap to her face, so stronger verbiage might scare her away. And he'd agreed that she could set the pace of their courtship. Should he wait for her to declare her love first? Would she ever?

His father rose as his mother entered, and he distributed plates of strudel, then took the tray and leaned it against the wall. "Looks scrumptious, my dear. Sit beside me over here."

They exchanged a look that Ernst could only describe as a caress, and he swallowed. Would his marriage to Ilsa be like theirs? His parents' love was deep and strong. They didn't blather on about their feelings, but they often shared glances, speaking volumes without saying a word. They also didn't cling to each other, but would often touch in passing: his mother brushing her hand on his father's sleeve or his father stroking his mother's hair. And the man could still make her blush as if she were a young woman. How did he do that?

As anticipated, his father bumped his mother's arm, then nestled close. She giggled and jabbed him with her elbow. Ernst shook his head, then felt Ilsa's eyes on him. He looked up and shrugged. Didn't she remember their behaviors from the past? They hadn't changed in four years. He picked up his fork. "Mother, I don't believe you've ever told Ilsa how you and Father met."

"Really?" His mother cocked her head. "She'd not interested in that."

"Oh, I'd love to hear that story. My parent's marriage was arranged as I thought most people were back then."

His mother took a bite of strudel and chewed slowly, her eyes taking on a distant gleam. A smile tugged her lips as she obviously slipped into the past. She swallowed and focused on Ilsa. "I lost my own father at a young age, so it was just Mama and me while I was growing up."

Ilsa gasped. "I didn't know. How tragic."

"Sad, but she made up for it in many ways. She was an opera singer, a coloratura soprano. She had the highest and clearest voice of anyone I've ever heard. Well-sought after in Europe, she traveled extensively and took me with her. It was a grand adventure, and I loved it. Despite being a visiting performer, she was popular among the troupe members, and I was coddled and loved by them all."

"What a unique childhood. It's no wonder you're a music teacher."

His mother shook her head. "Mama would have preferred that I become a singer like herself. She groomed me and taught me everything she knew. When I was about twelve years old, I was given my first role, a tiny one with only a few measures of song, but I was hooked. I reveled in the applause, the glamor of the set and costumes, and the travel. Years went by, and I was awarded more parts. My voice had matured into what is called mezzo-soprano, not as high as Mama's, but well-developed. As was typical for mezzos, I was cast in the role of villainess or seductress. Soon, I was nearly as popular as Mama."

"What happened?" Dismay etched lines in Ilsa's face. "Was your mother upset about your success?"

"No, she was over the moon. By the time my achievements surpassed her own, she was ready to retire. Her voice was tired, and she was unable to sing the notes that made her famous. She took the occasional matronly role, but was satisfied with pushing my career forward." His mother slipped her hand into his father's. "Then I met Anton, and my life changed forever."

Ernst grinned. "This is the part where she talks about what a dashing young man he was. Handsome, sophisticated, and a bit of a rogue."

Ilsa gaped at his father who snickered and said, "She's always had a flair for the dramatic."

His mother lifted her chin. "Every woman should feel the same way about her man. Although not every mother wants her son to be considered a rogue."

"Don't worry, Mother. I'm on the straight and narrow." Ernst laid his fork on his empty plate. "Pray, continue."

"Yes, please." Ilsa's eyes glowed. "It all sounds very romantic."

"We fell in love at first sight." She patted his father's cheek. "He attended a performance in Munich, then showed up every night for a week, but always sitting in the back so I didn't see him. He tried to sneak backstage on a couple of occasions but was caught and unceremoniously thrown out. He finally resorted to bribing one of the ushers to hand me a note asking to meet. I was intrigued."

"Hadn't others tried to pursue you? Sent you notes?"

"Absolutely, but their words were disingenuous. I knew they only wanted to be associated with my money and fame." She sighed. "But Anton's message was different. He spoke of how my music blessed him. No one had ever said that. I knew my voice was a gift from God, and he recognized that. We met, and our hearts united. I knew he was the man God had chosen for me."

"And you gave up your career aspirations just to marry and have a family." Ilsa pressed her hand against her chest. "Astonishing."

"*Just to marry.*" His mother pursed her lips. "I didn't settle. One is not more important than the other. They are merely different. But I feel I have the best of both worlds, my dear. I teach music, and these two people love me more than anything. Traveling was exciting, but it was also lonely. I'm right where God wants me, and I'm more fulfilled than I would have been had I remained with the opera."

Ernst peeked at Ilsa who seemed mesmerized by the story. Would she be able to find the balance between career and family? Did she want to? Time would tell.

Chapter Twenty-Seven

Hunched over her desk, Ilsa glanced from the memo to her staff. Oblivious to the news in her hand, they smiled as they worked. The machines clattered in an off-beat rhythm, some of the women swaying to unheard music while others stood ramrod straight. She was more like the latter group, never able to relax while the apparatus was running. Once she'd learned there didn't seem to be one right way for the women to complete the task, she allowed them to complete the task in a way that was comfortable for them.

Zlata glanced at her and raised her hand in a quick wave. Ilsa nodded, then dropped her gaze to the offending missive. What was the best way to convey the information? Should she wait until break when they could talk about the decision among themselves? Or should she speak with them upon their return? Or now?

A sigh escaped, and she rubbed her throbbing forehead. She hated this sort of dilemma, but the bad came with the good, and it had been a while since she'd had tell the gals something they didn't want to hear.

Had Ernst known about this before dinner with his parents yesterday? The announcement arrived about an hour into her shift, so there was a chance he did. Why wouldn't he mention it to her? She twisted her lips. She'd made no bones about separating their business and professional lives, so even if he did know, he wouldn't have let the information intrude on their Sunday dinner. She had no one to blame but herself if he was withholding the report.

Maybe she should wait until the end of their shift. No, better to catch them before break. Otherwise, her staff would hear it from workers in other departments. Better for her to disseminate the announcement. Then she could set their mind at ease and answer any questions or concerns.

She checked the watch pinned to her jacket and pushed herself to her feet. Ten minutes until break. Putting her fingers between her lips, she whistled, a piercing sound that cut through the racket in the cavernous room. Tobias would be proud. He'd taught her how to create the shrill blast after she'd pestered him for days when she heard him in the schoolyard a year or so before Mama passed away. Her mother had admonished her that ladies didn't whistle, but every now and then the skill came in handy. Fortunately, there were no men around to be appalled, and Mama was gone.

She waved her arms, and the girls turned off their machines. They gathered around, a mixture of emotions in their eyes. "Thank you, everyone." She let her gaze rest on each girl for a brief second, then laced her fingers in front of herself. "I received a memo from Mr. Beck that the factory will be operating on Thanksgiving Day, and we will be expected to work."

Gasps and comments rippled through the group, and she held up her hands. "Quiet, please. I know you're upset. Frankly, I'd rather not work either. Thanksgiving is an important holiday, and most of us spend it with our families. The company received a large order from a new client, meaning a busy time just got busier. You'll, of course, be paid overtime for the work. After we make it through the new year, you'll all get an extra day off."

More grumbling and murmuring.

"Please address your questions and comments to me rather than complaining to your coworkers."

A voice from the back said, "It's this sort of nonsense that brings in the unions. We shouldn't have to work on a holiday. We get so few as it is."

"Mr. Beck must weigh the needs of the business with that of his employees. I'm sure he'd rather be with his family."

Harsh laughter punctuated the group, and Olya said, "You honestly believe he's going to work that day?"

Ilsa waved the memo. "According to this, he will be here."

"Still, we shouldn't have to work on one of our few days off."

"But you will be paid extra for the time." Ilsa pointed to the page. "One of the suggestions is to celebrate your Thanksgiving that night after work. Granted, the meal will need to be much simpler. No one will have time to cook a turkey, but the holiday is about family, not what you're eating."

Zlata grinned. "So, he's saving us money."

"That's one way to look at it." Ilsa sent her friend a grateful smile. "Or you can wait until Saturday to hold your Thanksgiving. Again, it's about being together, not about which particular day you celebrate." Surprised Yasmina hadn't made any negative comments, Ilsa searched the group for the woman. She stood in the back, arms crossed. At Ilsa's look, she shrugged. It would have been better to have her support, but neutrality worked, too.

The bell rang for break.

"This is a lot to take in, so feel free to ask me questions after you return or over the next few days. Enjoy your break, ladies, and try to understand that Mr. Beck must have felt he had no other option than to ask us to work."

The women muttered as they turned and made their way down the aisle, then out of the room. Silence descended, and Ilsa trudged back to her desk. She'd give the staff space to talk about the announcement rather than join them for break as usual. She opened the drawer and tossed the page inside. No need to look at it. She'd read it so often she'd memorized the missive.

She understood the girls' consternation. They did get very few days off. Mr. Beck was more generous than most employers as far as she'd been able to surmise, but he was a businessman first and foremost.

Her girls needed to remember that paying overtime was unusual in the business world as was the five-day week he'd instituted.

Time crawled as she waited for her workers to return.

Three minutes before they were due, Zlata hurried through the door. She glanced over her shoulder, the rushed to Ilsa's desk. "I'm taking a chance by talking to you, but I wanted you to know that some of the girls are talking about contacting the union representative, and others want to call in sick."

"Oh, no." Ilsa blew out a deep breath. "I'm not sure which is worse."

"Probably calling in sick. There's not enough time for the union to make any sort of difference, even if they could get voted in prior to the holiday."

"True. Do you have an idea of how many might participate?"

Zlata tossed another furtive look behind herself. "Maybe a third? I'm not sure. Most know we're close, so they kept their chatter to a minimum around me."

"I don't know for certain, but they could lose their jobs."

"I'll socialize that information." Zlata laid her hand on Ilsa's arm. "Don't say anything to anyone yet. With enough time, this could blow over."

"Or not."

"Please, Ilsa. Give me until Friday. I'll try to deter them."

Voices sounded in the hallway, and Zlata scuttled to her machine before anyone entered the room. She sent Ilsa a silent plea, then turned on her machine.

Ilsa sighed as she watched the women arrive, most quiet, but a few talking and sending her scathing looks as if the decision had been hers. Where did her loyalty lie? Should she notify upper management about the potential "sick day," or should she grant Zlata a reprieve to convince the women that staying home from work on Thanksgiving was a bad idea?

Chapter Twenty-Eight

With a grim smile, Ilsa pushed herself to her feet, then wended her way through the machines, periodically stopping to ask if the worker had any questions or comments because of the announcement. Most shrugged and shook their heads, but more than a few sneered or frowned in response. Zlata murmured encouragement. Ilsa sighed and went to the vacant machine she used during her shift. She needed to do something other than think.

Switching on the apparatus, she grimaced. She should be praying not worrying. What had Pastor Krueger said...joy *in spite of* circumstances. *Oh, Father, forgive me. I am too easily swayed by my emotions and situation. I get upset when things are hard or not going the way I planned. I want to do better. I want to be a light that leads others to You. I want to react in a Christlike manner, thinking first what He would do. Help me do right by my staff and the company.*

Peace settled over her like a blanket on a winter night, and she smiled. The issue hadn't been solved, but she wasn't alone. She never had been. Thankfully, God accepted her just as she was, blemishes and all. He forgave her inclination to rush forward, then beckon for Him to catch up.

No wonder she found herself in a quandary. Too bad she couldn't be more like Nadine...levelheaded and serene.

She let herself get lost in the tedious rhythm of the machine, her hands flying over the controls when necessary, and packing the wrapped bars into the carton as they emerged. Stacks grew quickly, and the box filled. She paused the machine, then swapped the brimming container for an empty one.

Hairs on the back of her neck prickled, and she lifted her chin, her gaze searching the room. At the end of the next aisle, one of the newer women watched, her expression impassive. Ilsa knew little about her, but during the interview she'd seemed eager to learn and contribute to the company's success. Had the announcement about working the holiday changed that for the woman? Had her initial excitement been contrived? Was she a union plant?

Out of foil sheets, the machine paused, breaking Ilsa's reverie. Was she seeing agitators where there weren't any? She switched off the apparatus, then walked to Zlata's station. "I need to get more wrappers, and I'm going to see Ernst. Please keep an eye on things while I'm gone."

Her friend nodded, her face clouded. "I understand. Hopefully, a solution will be found the employees can accept. I don't want to be part of calling in sick, but I am torn about what to do."

Tamping down feelings of guilt, Ilsa hurried from the room. Zlata might be conflicted about her loyalty, but Ilsa was not. She worked for Mr. Beck, and he paid her salary. Her allegiance must lie with him. She liked most of her employees, but she was their boss, not their friend. She must do her small part to ensure the founder had all the information he needed to run the company.

She strode past doorway after doorway, each department emitting its unique sounds from machinery. In between break time, the corridors were empty, and her shoes slapped loudly on the wooden floors. Would Ernst be available? She should also tell Mr. Johnstone, her direct supervisor. Her steps wavered. She should see him first, or she would confirm the speculation that Ernst was someone special to her. The men sat near each other, so she'd collar them both.

One final turn, and she arrived in the administrative section of the factory. No clatter or banging from machines peppered the air. Instead, the low murmur of voices, and the occasional sound of a drawer closing wafted toward her.

Forcing herself forward, she read the names on the doors to find Mr. Johnstone's office. *Please let him be in.* At the far end of the hall, her ears pricked up. Ernst's voice. She was getting closer. Two doors down, and there was Mr. Johnstone's name. She peeked inside and smiled. The two men were together standing close to a large chart pinned to the wall. Intent upon their work, neither one saw her, so she rapped on the doorframe. They turned, and Ernst's face lit up.

Mr. Johnstone looked concerned. "Miss Krause, what brings you here? Is everything all right?"

"May I come in? There's something you need to hear. Both of you."

Ernst motioned toward a chair near the desk, worry lines appearing on his forehead. "About the Thanksgiving announcement?"

"Yes." Ilsa frowned. "How did you know?"

"There have been lots of rumblings this morning." Mr. Johnstone crossed his arms. "More so than anticipated."

She sank into the chair and wrapped her arms around her middle. "How can you be surprised? Thanksgiving is an important holiday to many, and we get few days off. To take one away, even with the promise of payment has caused dismay."

"True." Ernst nodded. "Do you have anything specific or are you simply reporting unrest?"

"Something *very* specific...a barrage of women calling in sick." Her gaze bounced between the two men. "One of my employees returned early from break and indicated that some of the girls talked about calling in that day, claiming to feel unwell."

"Disappointing. Mr. Beck hoped that employees would understand the business need and be willing to work. They *are* being paid." Ernst rubbed his jaw. "And he'll be giving up his holiday, too."

"I told them, but that didn't seem to matter. I guess they only care about themselves."

Mr. Johnstone said, "As do most people, Miss Krause."

Her cheeks scorched. "Of course. I didn't mean—"

"I wasn't reprimanding you, just stating a fact." Mr. Johnstone sent her a tired smile. "Ernst here has already been to see Mr. Beck and suggest that our founder consider allowing staff to choose whether to come in or not."

"But won't that result in fewer people working?"

"Not necessarily." Ernst shook his head. "I read an article once about charitable giving during events. Some studies have shown that asking for a suggested donation rather than mandating a ticket price often leads to higher contributions. If we give staff control over the situation, they may feel more generous, as it were."

"When did Mr. Beck promise an answer? I'd like the women to know before they go home tonight."

"Later this afternoon." Mr. Johnstone glanced toward the large clock above the chart. "He made the same observation."

Ernst patted her shoulder. "I think Mr. Beck is going to accept the recommendation. He seemed to be leaning in that direction when I left his office. He commented that family is more important than business. He also pointed out that employees shouldn't necessarily be impacted by poor planning on the part of a customer."

Relief coursed through her. Ernst's idea was intriguing. He was smart being able to extrapolate the information from the article to the situation in the factory. Would she have been able to make that kind of connection? She hadn't enjoyed being the bearer of bad news and handling the conflict. And she could relate to her employees' dismay. She didn't want to work Thanksgiving Day either. Did her agreement with the staff mean she was more like them than management? Should she step down? The higher salary was a tremendous help toward paying down the debt, but was it worth the heartache associated with leading others? She'd be glad when she didn't *have* to work. What would that be like?

Chapter Twenty-Nine

Arms full of wrapping foil, Ilsa made her way back to her station. Hours had passed since talking with Ernst and Mr. Johnstone, and she'd refilled her machine twice. She didn't normally work on the line this long, but the steady cadence of the apparatus had soothed her agitation. She should have known the upper-level managers would have known about the unrest. That they would have discussed the situation and come up with solutions. When would Mr. Beck make his decision? The day was nearly over.

She surveyed the room. As time elapsed, tension thickened in the room. Returning from their afternoon break, the girls had seemed more tense than when they'd left. They also seemed more...resigned...resolved. She searched her mind for the right word to describe the aura surrounding the women. Even Zlata seemed off-kilter. She'd huddled close to her machine, and only looked at Ilsa once. She wouldn't put the woman on the spot by approaching her, but did she know something?

Mr. Johnstone entered the room waving a sheaf of papers, a broad grin on his face. "Miss Krause, I have excellent news." He rushed toward her. "Mr. Beck has amended his earlier decision. Here is the official announcement, but the crux of it is that he's agreed to Mr. Webber's suggestion of making the day voluntary. Your staff may choose to come in for a full or half day. As mentioned, they will be paid overtime for any hours worked and will be given an additional full or half day off in January, based on their Thanksgiving shift."

"That's wonderful, Mr. Johnstone." Ilsa clapped her hands. "I'll tell the girls right away."

He handed her one of the pages. "Perfect. I cannot stay. I must inform my other departments."

"Absolutely."

With a quick nod, he rushed down the aisle and out the door.

She turned toward the machines. Most of her staff was already looking in her direction, so she gestured for them to join her. It didn't take long for them to gather in a circle around her. Hoping to wipe the suspicious and guarded expressions from their faces, she gave them her brightest smile. "I'm pleased to announce that Mr. Beck has amended his decision requiring us to work on Thanksgiving."

A collective gasp swept over the group, and some of the girls applauded.

"The work still needs to get done, so he is *asking* folks to come in and work. Half-day and full-day shifts are available. You'll be paid the overtime as previously promised as well as given time off in January commensurate to the hours you work on the holiday." She waved the sheet. "I'll post this on the wall for your perusal, but isn't that great news?"

Several of the women nodded, relief obvious. Others continued to scowl. Now, what?

She tilted her head. "Some of you still seem bothered. Does this not solve your problem about working the holiday? You don't have to if you don't want. I thought you'd be happy."

"We shouldn't have to choose." A voice came from the back.

"I don't understand." Ilsa craned her neck to see who'd spoken. "By allowing you to decide, Mr. Beck is giving you an option."

"The choice creates more problems." Yasmina raised her hand. "If I don't work, I'll be causing problems for my coworkers, and I would feel bad about that. If I do work, my family will be mad at me for choosing to be away from them. Also, will I be looked down on if I don't work? Is this a trick? Is Mr. Beck testing our loyalty? Will those who work be considered better employees than those who don't?"

"All very good questions, Yasmina." Ilsa tapped her chin with one finger. "First of all, I don't think this is a ploy. I spoke with Mr. Johnstone and Mr. Webber and was told that Mr. Beck recognizes the importance of family time and holidays. He wants you to do what is best for you and yours. Secondly, I don't know about others, but I will not look down upon you, should you stay home."

Some of the girls murmured.

"Personally, I'm going to discuss this with my siblings and ask them to celebrate on another day. I don't know your situations, but I would hope your family cares enough about you to be flexible. If they are not, you're welcome at my table, and I will let you know what day we'll be holding our holiday." She blinked. The offer had come out of her mouth unbidden, but she realized she meant it. "Are there other comments or questions?"

No one said anything, so she motioned toward the machines. "We only have a short time before the end of the day. Most of you are feeling unsettled, so do the best you can."

As the women returned to their stations, her shoulders sagged. There were definitely days she wished she still merely worked the line. Or even better, the farm.

Movement in the doorway caught her eye. Three men entered the room, their faces masks of anger and disdain. They produced guns, and two of them rushed down the aisle, the other man remaining in place to block the exit. She sucked in a breath. Who were they, and what did they want? Did they plan to kill everyone? She swallowed against the nausea swirling in her stomach. *Dear Lord, save us!*

Several of the girls screamed, while others moved to hide behind their machines.

Ignoring the workers, they stopped in front of Ilsa. "You." The man in front, short, stocky, and swarthy, pointed the gun at her chest. "You're the supervisor in here, right?"

"Yes." Her voice caught, and she cleared her throat. "Yes, I am. What did I do to deserve such treatment?" Under her skirt, her knees trembled, her strong words bravado.

"I'm the one asking questions, not you." He sneered at her. "Where are the others?"

"The other what?"

He pressed the weapon against her sternum. "Don't get cute."

"I'm not." She clenched her fists. "Shoot me if you must, but I don't understand the question."

"You are a stupid one, aren't you?" He smirked. "I'll talk slow so you get it. Where. Are. The. Other. Managers?"

She narrowed her eyes at the man. She'd never seen him before. Where did he work? "There are three of us, one per shift. I am the only one assigned to work here during the day. So, I'm assuming the others are at home."

"Fine, but if I find out you're lying..." An ugly laugh burst from his lips. "Let's just say it won't go well for you."

"I'm not lying." She spoke through gritted teeth.

He grabbed her arm in a vicelike grip, sending pain shooting to her shoulder. She tried to pull away, but his hold was too tight. "A feisty one." He leered at her, then exchanged a glance with his cohort and shoved her at the man. "Take her to the others. I've got one more stop."

The man poked her in the side with his pistol. "Come on, lady. We ain't got all day."

She flinched and forced her quivering legs to move. Each time she slowed down, he prodded her with the muzzle. Her heart thudded in her chest, and her palms were slick with sweat. He marched her to the administration section of the facility and flung open the door to one of the large meeting rooms. Three men stood near the entrance, their weapons trained on a dozen or so managers, most of whom she recognized. Ernst was in front, and her pulse skipped. He was here, safe and sound, but that also meant he wasn't on the outside able to rescue them.

Her guard thrust her toward the group, and she stumbled. Ernst rushed forward to catch her. His arm slipped around her waist, and she wilted against him. "Who...how?"

His embrace tightened. "They're farmers."

"What?" Her gaze went back to the gunmen. "But why?"

"We don't know yet. They haven't given us their demands. Fortunately, it appears they haven't been able to locate Mr. Beck."

"How did they get inside?" Her eyes widened. "The front desk..."

"There were no shots, so we're hopefully no one was hurt."

"What are we going to do?"

"Be quiet!" one of the captors barked and waved his weapon. "No talking, or else."

Ilsa clamped her lips together. *Why had God allowed this to happen?*

Chapter Thirty

Narrowing his eyes while he surveyed their captors, Ernst pulled Ilsa closer. Her warm body trembled, but she'd regained her outward appearance of composure. She stood tall and glared at the gunmen. Behind him, a couple of the female managers sobbed quietly. How much longer would the group be detained? Would the abductors carry through with their threats of shooting anyone who gave them problems? What had driven the men to this level of desperation?

The door opened, and a short, beefy man shoved another one of the first-level managers into the room before meeting the gaze of the tallest of their captors and jerking his head toward the corridor. Both men slipped outside, and the door closed again. The newest manager gaped at them before he was shoved from behind and stumbled forward. He turned and snarled at the man who'd jabbed him, then stalked to the wall. He crossed his arms and looked mulish. Ernst sighed. He knew how the man felt, but to antagonize their jailers might prove dangerous.

Time crawled, and Ernst continued to study the two remaining gunmen. He'd seen both around town but didn't know their names. Somewhere in their thirties, they wore clean but ragged denim pants and flannel shirts. The man in the blue shirt had long hair tied back with a leather strap. Taller, the other man had closely shorn white-blond hair, making him appear bald. They talked between themselves, their weapons dangling loosely from their hands.

Ernst counted the number of captives...seventeen, twelve of whom were men. Could they take the guys by surprise and overpower them? He poked Oxford, then rolled his eyes toward the men. Oxford blanched and shook his head. Would any of his colleagues be willing to take a chance? Was the potential loss of life worth the risk?

Noise sounded in the hallway, and the third man returned to the room. Heavily mustached, he appeared to be the oldest of the three. His face was deeply tanned and lined, his hair more salt than pepper. He was also better dressed than the other two, his clothing clean and new-looking. Rather than a pistol, he carried a rifle, a high-end Winchester. He apparently had money. Why had he thrown in his lot with the others?

Rich Guy smirked at the group, then turned to the pair and said something under his breath. They straightened their spines, tightened the grip on their weapons, and faced the managers.

Heart pounding, Ernst pushed Ilsa behind him. He would die before allowing them to shoot her. But first, he'd make an effort to reason with them. He raised his hand and sent what he hoped was a confident look at Rich Guy.

The man's left eyebrow shot up, and he strolled toward Ernst, Winchester propped on his shoulder. "Fancy yourself a brave one?"

Ernst lifted his chin. He would not be cowed by these men, but he wasn't foolish enough to irritate them. "Not particularly, but I would like some answers if you'd be so kind. We've been here for hours, and I think we deserve to know what's going on."

Staring at him for a long moment, the man finally broke eye contact and laughed, an ugly, sinister sound. "You people don't deserve anything."

"I'm simply trying to understand what you expect to achieve by all this. We can't help you unless you tell us what you want."

"You that important? You got pull with the great Mr. Beck?" Rich Guy grabbed him with one hand by the front of his jacket and yanked him close. Face inches from Ernst's, he shouted, "Or are you lying in an effort to save your skin?"

"Believe what you want." Ernst shrugged and willed his thundering heart to stop racing. He tried to affect a bored persona. "Standing around isn't accomplishing anything, and the longer you keep us, the more time the authorities have to come up with a plan to thwart you. Is that what you want? You regret this little escapade? Or are *you* not as important as you're leading us to believe? You gotta wait for the *big man* before making a move?"

"Ernst." Ilsa's voice was a mixture of warning and fear.

"You might want to listen to your girlfriend." Rich Guy released him and stroked the muzzle of the rifle. "You don't want to make me angry."

"You're already angry." Ernst smoothed his jacket. "But unless your only goal is to frighten a bunch of innocent people, your little coup isn't too successful. Whatever you think Mr. Beck has done or not done can be addressed. For example, he mandated working on Thanksgiving. After a number of employees expressed their displeasure, he reconsidered and has made working that day voluntary. He's a reasonable man. He recognizes the importance of family and a quality life."

"Bah! Reasonable. Not in the least."

"Have you tried to meet with him and present your concerns?"

Rich Guy's face clouded, but he remained silent.

"Just tell me what he did that was so awful." Ernst spread his hands. "And then I'll shut up."

"Promise?" Rich Guy snickered, a glimmer of admiration in his eyes.

Ernst smiled. "To be honest, if I think I can help solve your problem, probably not."

The man threw back his head and guffawed. His cohorts chuckled, but remained vigilant. The managers murmured, and a few giggled nervously. Rich Guy's laughter died down, and he relaxed his hold on the gun. "I like you. You seem a decent guy. All right. I'll tell you what's going on. Since mid-October, your Mr. Beck has been lowering the amount of money he's paying per gallon of milk. Two days ago, he cut the price by ten percent. It's the busiest time of year when he's making buckets of profit. It takes a hard-hearted man to do something like that."

Turning to Ilsa, Ernst frowned. "Has Tobias said anything to you about this?"

"No. In fact, he continues to claim the farm is doing better than ever."

"Hmm. Maybe he's making up the difference with crops."

"But why didn't he tell me?"

"Who is Tobias?" Rich Guy glowered. "He a friend of yours?"

"He's my brother, and he has a contract to supply milk to Mr. Beck."

"Maybe Mr. Beck is only changing the price for those of us who don't have family members who work for him."

"That makes no sense." Ernst rubbed the back of his neck. "And it would be highly unethical."

"Your point?" Rich Guy sneered. "Your illustrious founder doesn't seem to have any ethics."

"No, he is an honorable and upright man. There must be another reason for this."

"How come you didn't know about the price changes? I thought you could help me."

"I believe I can." Ernst squinted at him. "You haven't done Mr. Beck any harm, have you?"

"What kind of man do you think I am?"

"One who carries a gun."

"I want to be taken seriously."

"Believe me. You are. Now, let's go see Mr. Beck and put an end to this. He might even agree not to press charges."

Rich Guy huffed out a loud breath and finger-combed his hair. "Fine. Let's go." He eyed the man with the ponytail, then jerked his thumb at Ilsa. "If we're not back in thirty minutes, kill her."

Chapter Thirty-One

Swaying, Ilsa moaned as her vision tunneled. Pinpricks of light twinkled as she fought to keep from fainting. Kill her? They'd kill her? How could the man say that after seeming to have a civil conversation with Ernst?

Ernst enveloped her in an embrace, then led her to one of the chairs where he lowered her into the seat. He shook his fist at the well-dressed man. "You've no reason to go that far. I've already said we'll work toward a solution."

"I'm simply trying to motivate you to work faster."

"Faster doesn't mean better." Ernst stroked Ilsa's shoulder. "You seem an educated man. I don't understand your need to bully and threaten us."

"You've not walked in my shoes."

"Nor have you walked in mine or any of theirs. What makes you think you have the most difficult life of everyone here?"

Pushing away Ernst's hand, Ilsa shot a silent plea heavenward as she climbed to her feet. She stuffed her cold hands into the pockets of her jacket. Would God save her? Did He have a bigger plan that included her death or that of the others? Whatever the plan was, she was done with sitting around in fear. God would work things to His glory. "Enough, gentlemen. Go. Find Mr. Beck and have your conversation. You have a roomful of frightened people who would like to go home to their families." She leveled her gaze on the man. "And I'm sure you would, too."

"The woman speaks." The tall man looked down his nose at her. "Such bravery from one so small."

Bible verse after Bible verse edged their way into her mind. God was reminding her of His presence and His power. "I may be little, but the God I serve is bigger than any of us." She cocked her head. "But you know that because I've seen you at church. Just once, this past Christmas, where you would have heard the message about our heavenly Father, and His love for us."

Beside her, Ernst drew in a sharp breath. She laid her hand on his arm to prevent him from speaking.

"God has nothing to do with this, so keep your sermonizing to yourself."

"As you wish." She dipped her head, then stroked Ernst's jaw with her thumb. "Go. Do your best and don't worry about how long the negotiations take. I'll be praying. Remember, God is in control, not these people. And if they do kill me, you're not to seek retribution. These men need God's mercy, and what better way to show it than to forgive their actions."

"I don't deserve you." Ernst brushed his lips on hers. "But I love you more than you'll ever know."

Her pulse thrummed. She didn't know what the next moment would bring, but she now had the assurance that Ernst loved her. "And I love you."

The man let out a derisive snort. "How sweet. Come on. Time is wasting."

They left the room, and Ilsa's knees gave way. She sank into the chair, the feel of Ernst's mouth on hers sending a tingle down her spine. Not only had he declared his love, but he'd kissed her in front of their colleagues. She waited for the waves of anxiety and consternation to fill her, but the emotions didn't materialize. She smiled to herself. She'd shed her immature notion that their relationship was unprofessional...something taboo that shouldn't be shared.

Miss Branche from the labeling department knelt beside her. "Thank you for what you said...about God. I needed to hear that. I've been waffling about becoming a believer since attending church three weeks ago." Her face glowed. "He is in control, isn't He?"

"Yes, He is." She laced her fingers with the woman's. "And you can ask Him into your heart this minute. You don't have to be in church or with a pastor."

"I don't?"

"No, God meets you where you are." Out of the corner of her eye, she saw their captives perk up. Were they listening to her conversation?

Of course they were. Everyone had ceased talking. She gulped. She was not a preacher or a missionary. She'd never presented the Gospel to anyone, especially to men who had the power to kill her. *Dear Lord, give me the words!*

"How can He do that if He hates us doing bad things?"

Ilsa licked her lips. "He hates what we do, but He doesn't hate us, and frankly, I don't understand how He does it because from what I know, He can't be in the presence of sin, but He will hear you when you cry out to Him and ask forgiveness." She huffed out a breath. What a rambling way to share the message. Now, she understood Moses telling God to pick his brother, Aaron, to speak. "I'm sorry if I'm confusing you."

"You're not, but I'm not sure how to pray and talk to God." Miss Branche's lips trembled. "I don't want to get this wrong."

"Just speak to Him as if you're talking to me. Share what's in your heart. I assure you. He will hear you."

"All right." She pulled her hand from Ilsa's and pressed her palms together, then bowed her head. "Um, God, it's me, Mavis. Thanks for loving me. I'm sorry for all the bad things I've done. Please forgive me. I want You in my life. Forever." She raised her head, and her eyes shimmered. "Is that good enough?"

"Of course. You feel different. You feel Him, don't you?"

"Yes." The woman chortled as she peeked at their captors. She whispered, "I can't believe they let you tell me about God. But I'm glad they did."

Ilsa leaned toward her and spoke out of the corner of her mouth, "They seemed to be listening. Perhaps He is touching them. We must pray that we've at least planted seeds."

"Fifteen minutes to go, missy. While you're praying, you better ask that God of yours for a resolution upstairs."

Chapter Thirty-Two

Perspiration beading at his hairline, Ernst strode through the corridors of the factory, Rich Guy on his heels. Who was he? An armed man stood at the doorway of each department, keeping workers inside. So many farmers. Were they all unhappy and feeling taken advantage of? How had things gotten this out of hand?

The silence from lack of machinery noise was deafening. Production numbers would suffer, but that seemed negligible in light of the possible loss of life.

He sighed and picked up his pace, finally arriving in the executive area of the facility. Another gunman waited outside Mr. Beck's office. Did the authorities know what was happening? Could the captives count on a rescue, or did the resolution lie solely with the conversation he was about to have with the founder? His palms moistened. *Lord, only You can intervene and bring a peaceful resolution. Please lay Your hand on all of us. Let us live to see another day.*

"Open the door."

With a nod, Ernst twisted the handle. He walked into the office, then froze.

Looking every bit the successful businessman, Mr. Beck sat at his desk, papers littering the surface. A crease in his forehead was the only indicator of his emotions. The man would make an excellent poker player.

"Sir." Ernst hurried forward. "How are you? You seem unharmed."

"Yes." Mr. Beck's gaze flicked to the gunman. "Ah, Mr. Satterfield. It's been a while. Do you represent the farmers' interests?"

Ernst gaped at his boss. The man seemed undaunted at the gunman's presence. When had they last met? What had happened? How could he remain so calm?

"I do, and I've brought Mr. Webber with me. He seems to think he can talk some sense into you about the situation."

Mr. Beck leaned back and steepled his fingers. "Good, because frankly, this has gone on long enough." His tone hardened. "It's bad enough you're holding me hostage in my own factory, but my people don't deserve such treatment. You better have a legitimate reason for this nonsense."

"Nonsense?" Satterfield jabbed his finger toward Mr. Beck. "Nonsense? You call cutting the amount of money you pay us for milk nonsense?"

"What?" Mr. Beck leapt to his feet. "What are you talking about?"

"Sit down!" Satterfield pointed the rifle at the founder. "And don't pretend you don't know anything about this."

Holding his hands up as if in surrender, Mr. Beck dropped back into the chair. He gestured to the chairs in front of his desk and sighed.

"Please put away your gun and join me. Both of you. Let's discuss this rationally. I haven't lowered what I'm paying for milk. That would require a new contract."

"Yeah, and we got one."

Ernst's neck swiveled back and forth between the two men. Had this debacle occurred because of a misunderstanding?

Mr. Beck's eyebrows shot up. "Not that I signed."

"You're lying. I have the contract right here." Satterfield cocked his head, and his grip on the weapon tightened. With the other hand, he reached into his pocket and withdrew a folded page. He tossed the paper on the desk. "Explain that."

Mr. Beck's gaze dropped to the contact, and his face reddened as he read. His fingers traced the cursive letters of the signature, and a muscle in his jaw jumped. He raised his head. "This isn't my signature." He straightened, then poked the page with his index finger. "I don't know who signed this, but I surely didn't. We've both been duped, Mr. Satterfield."

"How do we find out who did this, Mr. Beck?" Ernst gulped. "We don't have time for a full investigation. Mr. Satterfield here has given orders for Ilsa to be shot if we're not back in"—he whipped out his pocket watch, then popped it open—"six minutes." He swung his head toward Satterfield as he stowed his timepiece. "You've got to rescind your command while we try to figure this out. We need to go right now. It will take us three or four minutes to return to the room."

"Come." Satterfield clambered to his feet and made it to the door in four long strides. Ernst and Mr. Beck followed him, and they rushed down the hall.

Ernst's breath was ragged in his ears, and a stitch pierced his side as he jogged through the factory. *Please, God, let us get there in time.*

They arrived at the meeting room, and Satterfield knocked, then called out, "Bernie, it's me. I'm coming in."

He opened the door, and the trio barreled inside. The two guards leaned against the wall while the managers cowered in the corner. Ernst bolted past Satterfield and wrapped his arm around Ilsa's shoulder. His heart banged in his chest, and he nearly wept. She was safe.

"What gives, boss?" The man in blue narrowed his eyes. "Did ya get him to change the contract?"

"Turns out it's a fake. There is no new contract."

Confusion and elation danced across Bernie's features as his gaze bounced from Satterfield to Mr. Beck. "We shoulda been paid the old rate this whole time?"

"Yep."

"And I will make things right, young man." Mr. Beck stepped forward. "We'll get to the bottom of this fraudulent act, but you and your colleagues will not have to suffer because of it. My man, Mr. Webber here, will conduct an immediate audit to determine how much money we owe you. Would you be kind enough to give us a week?"

"Well, yeah!"

Satterfield slapped him on the shoulder and grinned.

One of the managers clapped his hands, then several others joined in until the room was echoing with applause. Mr. Beck beamed and extended his arm to Satterfield, who accepted the gesture, shaking the founder's hand with vigor.

Movement in the back of the group caught Ernst's attention, and he shifted to get a better glimpse. Mr. Geld, the company's accountant put his hands on his hips and glared at the two men. Brows furrowed, his face was dark with displeasure. How could the man be upset that the situation had been resolved?

A chill slithered up Ernst's spine. Was he responsible for the misdeed? Next to the company attorney, the man was in the best position to execute a plan such as this. Ernst whispered into Ilsa's ear, "I think I've discovered our culprit."

"What? Who?" She craned her neck to search the group.

"Shh. Don't look."

Too late. Geld met Ernst's look, and his face darkened. He uncrossed his arms and reached into his jacket. At the glimmer of steel, Ernst elbowed his way through the crowd toward the man. "No!" He reached toward the man, hands grappling to push him to the floor.

An explosion sounded, then screaming. Searing pain like a hot poker burned in his shoulder. The acrid stench of gunpowder filled his nose. His steps faltered, and he pitched forward. As he fell, he made contact with Geld and shoved him to the floor. They rolled and tumbled,

Ernst grabbing for the gun a short distance away. Blood poured from the wound, soaking his jacket. His vision wavered. He had to secure the weapon before he passed out.

"It's all right, Mr. Webber. We've got him." The voice seemed to come down a long tunnel, and Ernst squinted into the light to see who'd spoken. "We've got the gun, too."

"Ernst." Ilsa dropped to her knees beside him, her wan face streaked with tears. "The doctor is coming." She stripped off her jacket, wadded it into a tight ball, and pressed the fabric against his shoulder.

Blazing agony engulfed him, and he moaned.

"I'm sorry, darling." Her fingers stroked his forehead, then she bent and brushed her lips on his. "But we've got to stop the bleeding."

He grunted, then cracked his eyelids. "Darling?"

Her face pinked. "Well, we did declare our love for each other."

"That we did." He grimaced. "And as soon as the doc has stitched me up, I'd hazard a guess that we can start courting officially."

She winked. "I'd say we've already begun."

Epilogue

Dressed in her petticoats and heart fluttering, Ilsa turned as the door opened with a creak. Her arms filled with a huge bouquet of hothouse roses, gardenias, and lilies, Nadine stepped into the room, Mrs. Beck close behind. Both wore broad smiles that faltered at her appearance. She shrugged. "I know. I should have already put on my gown. Can you help me?"

"Of course, my dear." Mrs. Beck approached, hands fluttering in the air like agitated butterflies.

Nadine laid the flowers on a nearby table, then rushed toward her. Eyes glimmering with tears, she met Ilsa's gaze in the mirror. "I thought this day would never come."

Ilsa laughed. "Ernst said the same thing last night."

"To everything there is a season, and a time to every purpose under heaven." Mrs. Beck lifted the lemon-yellow dress from the rocking chair and handed it to Nadine. "Besides, your wedding should not have been shuffled between the events of these last few months."

"True." Nadine nodded. "Raise your arms."

Complying, Ilsa sighed as her sister slipped the satiny material over her head. Soft as goose down, the fabric settled on her hips. She poked her arms through the cap sleeves. "Mr. Beck was very generous in not bringing charges against the farmers. It's too bad the law required them to be charged by the state."

Nadine buttoned the dress, then smoothed Ilsa's skirt. She picked up the circlet of flowers and pinned them in Ilsa's upswept hair. "Yes, but he appeared at the trial on their behalf and convinced the judge to sentence them to doing chores for the community rather than sending them to jail after the guilty verdict. So, the situation turned out as well as can be expected. There doesn't seem to be any lasting bad feelings."

"My Wilhelm has always been progressive. Taking the men away from their families would only have worsened the situation. The judge was wise enough to agree." Mrs. Beck tilted her head and studied Ilsa. "You are a beautiful young woman, but there is still something missing." She unclasped the diamond and topaz necklace from her neck and handed the strand to Nadine. "That should take care of something borrowed."

"Mrs. Beck, I can't wear this." Ilsa shook her head. "It's too valuable."

"Don't be silly. Of course you can. The gems are the perfect accent to your dress. Don't you agree, Nadine?"

"Yes, ma'am." Nadine fastened the jewels around Ilsa's neck. "Say thank you," she hissed.

"Thank you, Mrs. Beck," Ilsa's voice squeaked, and the women giggled.

Music sounded from deep inside the house. The moment had arrived. She would walk out the door and into the enormous living room and marry Ernst. Life had come full circle. Papa's debt had been paid in full, and yesterday had been her last day at work. She'd miss some of the girls, Zlata especially, but now that the woman had been promoted to take Ilsa's place, they'd be able to socialize without censure. She rolled her eyes. Foolish society rules, but she'd have minded them instead of causing Ernst problems in his new position. Mr. Beck had done a lot to create a close-knit community, but the old ways die hard.

Shaking her head to dispel the thoughts, Ilsa squeezed Mrs. Beck's arm. "And thank you for letting me get married in your gorgeous home."

"It's the least Wilhelm and I could do for you and your young man. If it wasn't for Ernst tackling Satterfield..." Mrs. Beck dabbed at her eyes with a gloved hand. "Well, you know what would have happened. Has Ernst's shoulder completely healed?"

"Yes, but the scar tissue still bothers him. The doctor gave him a cream to use, and we're hoping it will make a difference over time."

Another knock sounded. "Is the bride ready?"

"Come in." Mrs. Beck handed Ilsa the bouquet, then kissed her cheek as the door opened and Tobias entered.

Eyes bright, he whistled. "Get a load of you, sis. Ernst might just faint after he sees you."

"I look all right?" Her stomach buzzed as if filled with a swarm of bumblebees. "I was torn between this dress and the pink one."

"He'd marry you even if you wore a potato sack, but, yes, you're gorgeous." He chuckled, then sobered up. "I know it's a hard day for you with Mama and Papa not here, but they'd be real proud of you. And thanks for letting me take Papa's place, walking you down the aisle."

"I wouldn't have it any other way."

He grinned and looked pleased, then crooked his arm. "Now, enough talking. Let's not keep the man waiting."

Ilsa buried her nose in the flowers and inhaled deeply, then lifted her chin and marched forward, eager to wed the man she adored and to see what God had in store for the two of them. "No, let's not."

THE END

A Bit of History and Inspiration

Milton Hershey and his chocolate empire are the inspiration for *The Chocolate Chronicles*. *Love and Chocolate* tells Ilsa's story, but Nadine, Tobias, and Heddie will all get their turn to be heard.

Having been raised first in Maryland, then New Jersey, I lived close enough to the town of Hershey, Pennsylvania to be one of the more than four million annual visitors to Hershey Park. Unfortunately, at that young age I was not enamored with history enough to bother driving past his home or the other historical buildings that comprise the town. What I do remember is the aroma of chocolate that pervades the air even from miles away.

Born September 13, 1857 in Derry Township, Pennsylvania, Milton and his family were part of the Mennonite community. Life was difficult. His father was a dreamer, and relocated the family on several occasions in search of work. It was often left to Milton's mother to ensure her children had enough food. She raised chickens and sold eggs, churned butter and made corn brooms to sell. But despite her best efforts, sometimes Milton and his sister, Sarena, didn't have shoes or enough to eat. More sadness followed when Sarena died of scarlet fever in 1867.

At the age of twelve, Milton left school to help add to the family coffers. He could read and write and perform simple math. At first, he was apprenticed to a printer, but Milton was miserable, and the story goes that he purposely let his hat fall into the press so he could be fired. He went to work for Royer's Ice Cream Parlor and Garden, and his fate was sealed.

He eventually opened his own candy business, but the company failed. Undeterred, he opened another candy operation, but that also went bankrupt. Then he developed the process of manufacturing caramel using milk, and his Lancaster Caramel Company grew exponentially. By the early 1890s, he employed more than 1,300 workers. However, after attending the 1893 World's Columbian Exposition (Chicago World's Fair), chocolate peaked his interest. He sold Lancaster for $1 million and created the Hershey Chocolate Company. By mass-producing milk chocolate, he was able to bring a formerly luxury goods product to the general public.

In 1898, Milton met and married Catherine "Kitty" Sweeney, whom he met at a candy shop while delivering a caramel order. The marriage was a happy one, and Milton adored Kitty. Kitty suffered from health problems, and the union did not produce any children. The couple traveled extensively seeking cures for Kitty's health issues.

Rather than dwell on what they didn't have, Milton and Kitty used their immense wealth to bring prosperity and hope to others. They built a community around the factory, and employees could choose to rent or purchase the houses. A complete infrastructure was created that included shops, schools, churches, medical centers, and public transportation. In 1909, the Hersheys founded the Hershey Industrial School that provided housing and education to orphaned boys from the local Derry Township area.

Sadly, Kitty died in 1915. Three years later, Milton created the M.S. Hershey Trust where he endowed his entire fortune. The trust continues to operate, providing educational and cultural opportunities to the local community.

Milton wasn't perfect, and there are reports about the mistakes he made, and some of the ways he and the company stumbled through the years, but by all accounts, he was a generous man, giving a "leg up" to many who'd struggled during the economic depression of the Panic of 1893 that lasted through 1897.

On October 13, 1945, Milton Hershey passed away at the age of 88. His legacy continues to this day.

References

Hershey by Michael D'Antonio, Simon & Schuster, 2006

Images of America: Hershey by Mary Davidoff Houts and Pamela Cassidy Whitenack, Arcadia Publishing, 2000

The Chocolate Trust by Bob Fernandez, Camino Books, Inc., 2015

The Hershey Company/About Us: www.thehersheycompany.com, accessed April 4, 2024.

Acknowledgments

Although writing a book is a solitary task, it is not a solitary journey. There have been many who have helped and encouraged me along the way.

My parents, Richard and Jean Shenton, who presented me with my first writing tablet and encouraged me to capture my imagination with words. Thanks, Mom and Dad!

Scribes212 – my ACFW online critique group that got me started on this journey: Valerie Goree, Marcia Lahti, and the late Loretta Boyett (passed on to Glory, but never forgotten). Without your input, my writing would not be nearly as effective.

Eva Marie Everson – my mentor/instructor with Christian Writers' Guild. You took a timid, untrained student and turned her into a writer. Many thanks!

SincNE, and the folks who coordinate the Crimebake Writing Conference. I have attended many writing conferences, but without a doubt, Crimebake is one of the best. The workshops, seminars, panels, critiques, and every tiny aspect are well-executed, professional, and educational.

Special thanks to Hank Phillippi Ryan, Halle Ephron, and Roberta Isleib for your encouragement and spot-on critiques of my first books.

Paula Proofreader (https://paulaproofreader.wixsite.com/home): I'm so glad I found you! My work is cleaner because of your eagle eye. Any mistakes are completely mine.

Thanks to my Aces who provide information, encouragement, and support.

A special thanks to fellow author Terri Wangard for suggesting War's Unexpected Gift as a title.

A heartfelt thank you to my brothers, Jack Shenton and Douglas Shenton, and my sister, Susan Shenton Greger for being enthusiastic cheerleaders during my writing journey. Your support means more than you'll know.

My husband, Wes, deserves special kudos for understanding my need to write. Thank you for creating my writing room – it's perfect, and I'm thankful for it every day. Thank you for your willingness to accept a house that's a bit cluttered, laundry that's not always done, and meals on the go. I love you.

And finally, to God be the glory. I thank Him for giving me the gift of writing and the inspiration to tell stories that shine the light on His goodness and mercy.

Other Titles by this Author

Romance

Love's Harvest, Wartime Brides, Book 1
Love's Rescue, Wartime Brides, Book 2
Love's Belief, Wartime Brides, Book 3
Love's Allegiance, Wartime Brides, Book 4

Spies & Sweethearts, Sisters in Service, Book 1
The Mechanic & The MD, Sisters in Service, Book 2
The Widow & The War Correspondent, Sisters in Service, Book 3

Gold Rush Bride Hannah, Gold Rush Brides, Book 1
Gold Rush Bride Caroline, Gold Rush Brides, Book 2
Gold Rush Bride Tegan, Gold Rush Brides, Book 2

Dinah's Dilemma, Westward Home & Hearts Mail Order Brides
Rayne's Redemption, Westward Home & Hearts Mail Order Brides
Daria's Duke, Westward Home & Hearts Mail Order Brides
Ellie's Escape, Westward Home & Hearts Mail Order Brides

Vanessa's Replacement Valentine, Brides of Pelican Rapids
A Family for Hazel, Brides of Pelican Rapids

Legacy of Love, Keepers of the Light

A Bride for Seamus, Proxy Bride Series
A Bride for Keegan, Proxy Bride Series

Estelle's Endeavor, Thanksgiving Books & Blessings Series, Collection 5
Francine's Foibles, Thanksgiving Books & Blessings Series, Collection 6

Maeve's Pledge, The Suffrage Spinsters Series

Dial V for Valentine, You're On the Air Series
Dial S for Second Chances, You're On the Air Series

Love at First Flight
Love Found in Sherwood Forest
On the Rails: A Harvey Girls Story
A Love Not Forgotten
A Doctor in the House
War's Unexpected Gift

Mystery
Under Fire, Ruth Brown Mystery Series, Book 1
Under Cover, Ruth Brown Mystery Series, Book 2
Under Ground, Ruth Brown Mystery Series, Book 3

Murder of Convenience, Women of Courage, Book 1
Murder at Madison Square Garden, Women of Courage, Book 2

Non-Fiction
WWII Word Find, Volume 1

Let's Connect!

www.LindaShentonMatchett.com

www.facebook.com/LindaShentonMatchettAuthor

www.pinterest.com/lindasmatchett

www.linkedin.com/in/authorlindamatchett

https://www.goodreads.com/author_linda_matchett

https://www.bookbub.com/authors/linda-shenton-matchett

Interested in more historical fiction?
Visit http://www.lindashentonmatchett.com/p/books.html